There were tons of old photos. Virginia and her dog. Virginia and her little brother. Virginia blowing out the candles on her birthday cake. I turned the page.

"That's weird," said Sean. It was a class picture, Grade 7, with rows of scrubbed, smiling faces in their class-picture best. But one girl's face was scribbled out with pencil so hard it had torn through the paper.

I ran my finger over the list of names below the picture. "That must be Eleanor Thomas," I said.

And that's when the lights went out.

POISON APPLE BOOKS

THE GHOST OF CHRISTMAS PAST

by Catherine R. Daly

SCHOLASTIC INC.

To Seamus and Oonagh and our awesome
(and ghost-free) Christmas ski trip.

ISBN 978-0-545-48422-0

Copyright © 2012 by Catherine R. Daly
All rights reserved. Published by Scholastic Inc.
SCHOLASTIC, POISON APPLE, and associated
logos are trademarks and/or registered
trademarks of Scholastic Inc.

12 11 10 9 8 7 6 5 4 3 2   13 14 15 16 17/0

Printed in the U.S.A.   40
First printing, November 2012

CHAPTER ONE

"Mittens."

"Check."

"Ski jacket."

"Check."

"Ski pants."

"Check."

"Two pairs of long johns."

"Check."

I looked up from the packing list in my hand as my mother held up a pair of red long johns, folded them expertly, and placed them in my suitcase. I was about to go on my very first ski trip, and my mother wanted to make sure I wasn't missing a thing. Hence the checklist and the clothing inspection.

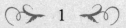

"You are one über-organized mama," I told her teasingly.

My mother looked up from the messy pile of clothes I had gathered and tucked her shortish brown hair behind her ears. "By failing to prepare . . ." she began.

". . . you are preparing to fail," I finished. Man! If I had a nickel for every time I had heard *that* one, I would be loaded. Personally, I'm more of a see-where-the-day-takes-you kind of girl. But I have to admit, when my mom is in charge, I always have everything I need, that's for sure.

"What's next?" she asked me.

"Ski goggles," I read.

My mother fished the goggles out of the pile and held them up. "Check."

"Three warm sweaters."

"Check, check, check," said my mom, carefully folding and packing them one by one. Did I mention she is an excellent packer?

"Seven pairs of warm so —" I started to read.

"Hey, what's this?" my mother interrupted me, holding up a floppy pink object made of rubber. She narrowed her eyes at me and shook her head. "Haley, I thought I had made this perfectly clear: No

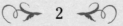 2

practical jokes on this trip. You are a guest of the McElhinneys and you need to be on your very best behavior."

I sighed and grabbed the whoopee cushion from her hand. It had been a birthday gift from my very best friend (and fellow practical-joke player), Lindsay McElhinney.

My mom continued. "That means no sneezing powder, no plastic wrap on the toilet seats. No caramel onions . . ." she added with a grimace.

I grinned. Lindsay and I considered the caramel onions we had created for Halloween to be our crowning achievement. They had looked so perfect, down to the sprinkling of nuts on top of the creamy caramel coating. When Lindsay's big sister, Olivia, had bitten into one, fully expecting to sink her teeth into a sweet apple and tasting the onion instead, she had literally wanted to kill us. But once she got past her initial red-hot anger, even *she* had admitted it was a brilliant prank. Jokes run in my blood, I guess. My dad is a prankster, and his dad taught him everything he knew. Even after my dad moved out and I was so upset I didn't want to speak to him, he could always get me talking by asking about the latest practical joke Lindsay and I had pulled.

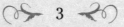 3

Lindsay had been begging me to join her family on their annual Christmas ski trip for years. I had always been tempted, despite the fact that I haven't skied since I was five, but I never wanted to leave my family around the holidays. Lindsay and I were closer than close. We had been best friends since, like, forever. We met in preschool when Frank Firestone stole my Tinky Winky doll and Lindsay marched right up to him and stole it back. I quickly discovered she was brave, funny, and totally unique. We hit it off immediately, becoming instant best friends.

Lindsay is a middle child, with a big sister and twin little brothers, Sam and Jack, who are seven years old. Since I am an only child, I spend a lot of time at her loud, busy house, so it's almost like I'm part of the family. I'd been hanging out at her house even more than usual the past couple of months, so when Lindsay, for the millionth time, asked me to come on the trip (this year to Snow City, an awesome ski town in the next state), fully expecting me to say my usual "Thanks but no thanks," I surprised us both by saying, "Sure, why not!"

My mom rolled up a pair of bright red-and-turquoise wool socks and tucked them into a corner of the suitcase. She sighed. "Unless of course you might change your mind about going away . . ." Her voice trailed off.

I gave my mom a sympathetic look and shook my head emphatically. But noticing the worried creases in her forehead, I added, "Of course I'm totally going to miss you. But skiing in Snow City over the holidays with Lindsay and her family? Too good to turn down."

My mom nodded sadly. We'd left the real issue unspoken between us, but it could have been written in neon lights on the orange walls of my bedroom: *This is the first Christmas since you and Dad split up, and I'd prefer not to be here for it, thank you very much.* Choosing which parent to spend Christmas Eve with and which one to spend Christmas Day with was too big a decision for one twelve-year-old to make. So I had opted for the easy way out — no decision at all. The fact that this still ended up causing hurt feelings all around did not escape my attention. But somehow it seemed easier this way.

So what if I hadn't skied since I was five? I'd learn. Lindsay was an expert skier, she was patient, and she had a whole week to teach me. And best of all — my BFF and I were going to be roommates for one week straight. Like the longest sleepover ever.

"I know you've got some trick up your sleeve for the holidays," my mom said as she rolled and packed the rest of the socks, carefully tucking them into the suitcase. "What do you and Lindsay have planned?"

I shook my head. "Honestly, Mom, nothing." I bit my lip. "Lindsay's been . . . um . . . a little distracted lately getting ready for the trip." I didn't mention what had been distracting her the most — the attention of the most popular girl in our class, Mackensie Martin.

It was weird — one weekend Lindsay and I were watching old *X-Files* episodes and plotting elaborate practical jokes, and the next she was dragging me to the mall to try on clothes and shoes and sit in the food court for hours on end to see if any boys from our class would walk by. Like it wasn't annoying enough to see them at school! We spent one entire Saturday on an elusive search for the correct shade of tangerine nail polish, believe it or not. I went along with her sudden obsession with fashion, fully convinced she would get bored with it and things would return to normal.

But then disaster struck — Lindsay showed up at school in a pair of leopard-print jeans that even I

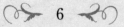

had to admit were pretty awesome and suddenly Mackensie was all over her, inviting her to sit at the popular girls' table at lunchtime and passing her notes in class that had a lot of smiley faces and LOLs on them. She and Mackensie had grown so close over the past month that, to my dismay, Lindsay had actually invited her along on the ski trip, too, even going so far as to tell her to bring whomever she wanted with her. And to my even greater dismay, Mackensie had accepted, inviting three of her clos- est friends along.

Lindsay's sudden interest in being popular was weird. She had never cared what anyone thought about her. I had been valiantly ignoring it, hoping it was a phase she was going through and that soon I would have my hilarious best friend back.

I was still waiting.

But now we would have a whole week together, being roommates and hanging out. And maybe, just maybe, Mackensie and her pals would actually be fun. There had to be something good about Mackensie and her posse for Lindsay to like them so much, I figured. Maybe I just needed to try a little harder to find out what it was. And as much as I hated to admit it, maybe a teeny-weeny piece of me hoped that some of their magic popularity dust would land on me.

Okay, I know I am an eternal optimist and that maybe I was reaching there. But it could happen, right?

"Haley!" Mom said. "Snap out of it! What's next on the list?"

"Three pairs of warm pajamas," I read.

No one can fold a pair of pajamas quite like my mother. Or fitted sheets — what's up with that? Impossible, right? Soon we were done packing. Satisfied that I would have everything I needed (and then some) for the week, Mom went to the kitchen to finish up dinner. I put on some music and filled my backpack with distractions for the long bus ride to the inn — a novel, a book of sudoku puzzles, my iPod with dozens of new downloaded songs (including the new Wild Flag album), and even a splitter so Lindsay and I could listen together. Plus a big bag of Sour Patch Kids to share. Lindsay couldn't resist the tart goodness of a Sour Patch Kid.

"Time for dinner!" my mom called. *Mmm.* We were having spaghetti and meatballs, my favorite dinner ever, in honor of my last night at home. I grabbed

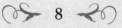

the whoopee cushion off my desk and slipped it into my suitcase, under a woolly sweater.

It was always better to be safe than sorry where practical jokes were concerned. You didn't want to get caught empty-handed when the perfect opportunity arose, that was for sure.

CHAPTER TWO

Normally, I hate waking up early. Hate, hate, hate it. But the next morning, my eyes snapped open even before my alarm went off. My stomach got that funny roller-coastery, nervous-but-excited feeling. Today was the day!

On most mornings, I would slap my alarm off disgustedly and my mom would have to call me two or three times (her voice rising more impatiently each time) to get me out of bed yawning and scowling. I am most definitely not a morning person. But my mom is always up at the crack of dawn, when she goes out for a run. Then she comes home and makes me breakfast, which is waiting for me every morning. When I finally haul myself downstairs, that is. Mom is a health-food nut, so there are no Pop-Tarts or

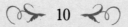

Froot Loops in my house; we're talking flax waffles, low-fat granola, and sheep's-milk yogurt. I am just like my dad, who finds it impossible to say a word to anyone until he has his first sip of coffee of the day. Sometimes I wonder if that is the real reason my parents split up. They are just on two different planets, time-wise.

But this morning was different. I got dressed quickly, ran a comb through my wavy, chin-length, dirty blond hair, and headed downstairs.

"You're up early," said Mom, not expecting a reply. She stood up from the table, where she had been reading the morning newspaper. "Oatmeal and strawberries?" she asked. I nodded and glanced at the paper. But I couldn't even feign interest in the news of the day, I was just too excited.

"So, I spoke to Gran and Gramps last night," Mom said, setting the bowl of oatmeal down in front of me. "They're looking forward to our Fake Christmas celebration when you return. Grandma's going to make a standing rib roast."

"Yum!" I said. "With the panties?" I loved that the little frilly things you put on the ends of the rib roast are called panties. I mean, what's that all about?

I took a big spoonful of oatmeal. "Are they still upset that I'm going away?"

Mom shrugged. "They'll get over it."

We grinned at each other. "Someday," we said in unison.

Despite my excitement, I managed to polish off the oatmeal, which was creamy and delicious. I brought the bowl over to the sink, rinsed it, and put it in the dishwasher.

My mom took a final sip and set down her mug of green tea. "Time to go!" she said brightly.

Mom was pretty quiet on the ride to Lindsay's. We had made this trip so many times in the past eight years, I was sure she could do it blindfolded. Meanwhile I fished around in my backpack for Lindsay's Secret Santa gift. Every Christmas, the McElhinneys did a huge gift exchange since there were so many of them, and I had gotten totally lucky by drawing Lindsay's name. I knew her gift was there, yet I felt compelled to make sure. It was just the most perfect gift ever, so I wanted to triple-check that I hadn't left it behind. My fingers grazed the slick wrapping paper and curly ribbon. Yes. There it was.

"Whoa," said Mom as we pulled up in front of Lindsay's house. "That is one huge bus."

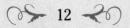

I stared at the large purple-and-blue bus with tinted windows that was parked at the curb. We were going skiing in style. Lindsay said her family did this every year. There were so many relatives going that it was cheaper to rent a bus than for everyone to drive separately and pay for gas. Plus, Lindsay said, this was way more fun.

I unsnapped my seat belt, grabbed the door handle, and hopped out eagerly. Mom followed, a little more slowly. I was in such a rush I nearly knocked myself over as I hauled my suitcase out of the trunk. A bunch of McElhinneys milled about, chatting, drinking coffee, and placing their suitcases, bags, and skis under the bus. I scanned the crowd, looking for my best friend. I stifled a giggle. Aunt Roberta, a large, cheerful, and flamboyant woman, had on a pair of strange boots made out of some white, long-haired animal fur that made her look like the Abominable Snowman from the knees down. I rolled my bag over to the side of the bus and the driver helped me stow it.

"Oh, look, there's Tina," said Mom, pointing to Lindsay's mom. I smiled. I love Lindsay's mom; she's so calm and sweet. She's like my second mother. We headed over to say hello.

"Hey, Haley," she said. "Can you believe this day is finally here?" She turned to my mom. "Stella!" she said, throwing her arms around her. "I still wish that you were coming, too."

My mom laughed. "As if my parents aren't freaking out enough already!" she said. She reached over and tousled my hair. "Take good care of my baby," she said. Normally I do not allow this kind of behavior, but I knew my mom was feeling sad, so I let her get away with it.

"She's an honorary McElhinney," said Lindsay's mom. "Don't worry about her one bit."

"So, where's Lindsay?" I asked.

She scanned the crowd. "She must already be on the bus," she replied vaguely.

She didn't wait for me? I wondered. *That's weird.*

I shrugged. I guessed Lindsay was excited for the trip to begin, too. I turned and gave my mom a quick hug. I didn't want any tears so I made it short and sweet. "See you next year!" I said lightly.

My mom bit her lip. "Have a safe trip, sweetie," she told me. "I'll miss you."

I walked over to the bus and turned around before I climbed up the stairs, giving my mom one last wave. Then I climbed on board. I was pleased to note that the bus was pretty fancy inside, with plush seats, footrests, tray tables, and TV screens. The bus was filled with people, most of whom I knew pretty well.

"Hi, Aunt Betsy," I said to a pretty woman with curly black hair.

"Haley!" she cried. "I didn't know you were coming. Now I know we're going to have fun!"

"Nice to see you, Boris," I said to her son, who was four. "And you too, Uncle Dave," I told his dad. I knew from experience that Boris was prone to loud and terrible tantrums when he did not get his way. I would make sure to sit far away from him.

Finally, I spotted Lindsay sitting by the window near the back of the bus. Her shiny dark brown hair was in a new hairstyle — bun pigtails. They looked very cute. *When did she start wearing her hair like that?* I wondered. I broke into a big grin and waved at my best friend. Lindsay waved back. I made my way to the seat, swung my backpack off my shoulder, and shrugged off my jacket.

"What's shaking, Princess Leia?" I said, about to sit down.

"Hello, Haley," said a voice. I turned around. To my disbelief and dismay, Mackensie slammed the

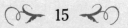

overhead compartment shut and shoved past me, plopping down in the seat beside Lindsay. That's when I noticed that she, too, was wearing her hair in bun pigtails. Lindsay liked to be different. She stopped wearing her favorite red patent leather Mary Janes when Tammy Collins bought the same pair. So that was kind of weird.

But what was even weirder was that Lindsay still hadn't told Mackensie that she was sitting in my seat and needed to move. I stared at Lindsay, but to my confusion, she just looked away uncomfortably.

I turned to Mackensie, who gazed at me smugly.

"Can I help you?" she asked obnoxiously.

"But . . . but . . . I thought you were sitting with Taylor," I said. Taylor was a member of Mackensie's clique. The two were joined at the hip, permanently. Brianna and Kaylee rounded out the popular group, and all four girls had never given me the time of day. They were too busy staring at themselves in any reflective surface they could find. In fact, at this very moment, Brianna and Kaylee were checking out their hair in the window across the aisle.

Mackensie shrugged. "Taylor can't come. She has the flu. So Lindsay agreed to be my travel buddy."

"But . . . but . . ." I was at a loss for words.

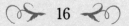

Lindsay finally made eye contact with me. Her eyes were saying, *I'm sorry*, while quietly begging me not to make a fuss.

As if in a daze, I slipped into the row behind Lindsay and Mackensie. There was nothing left for me to do. I sank into the seat and turned to the window. Through the space between the two seats I could see Mackensie's flaxen blond head lean toward Lindsay's dark brown one. The two started giggling.

I will not cry. I will not cry. I will not cry, I told myself harshly. Still, I felt the tears welling up, perilously close to falling as the bus started and I saw my mom blindly waving at the tinted windows. I suddenly wished I had been a little nicer to her when I had said good-bye.

The bus headed down the street and made a left at the STOP sign. We were on our way. For better or for worse.

I was counting on better, of course.

CHAPTER THREE

As we merged onto the highway, I took a deep breath and decided I was going to be the better person. So what if my best friend had abandoned me for the most popular girl in class? I could handle it. I fished into my backpack, my hand briefly and reassuringly, resting on the Secret Santa gift before settling on the paper bag containing my secret weapon. I stood up and popped my head over the seat in front of me.

"Hello, girls," I said. "Sour Patch, anyone?"

They both turned around to face me. I could see that they were sharing a gossip magazine featuring a spread devoted to the best and worst beach bodies. The page was covered with photos of celebrities and quasi-celebrities in their bathing suits. I averted my

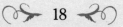

eyes. (The worsts were pretty bad.) That was surprising. Lindsay thought those celebrity magazines
were lame. But I could see that she was doing an
excellent job of looking fascinated.

"Yuck," said Brianna, chiming in from across the
aisle. "They're so *sour*," she added, making a face.

"Well, they are called *Sour* Patch Kids," I said
lightly. Brianna was not the sharpest knife in the
drawer; that was a known fact.

Lindsay smiled and reached for the bag.

"Gross," said Mackensie loudly, and Lindsay
instantly retracted her arm. "Aren't those, like, for
kindergartners?" she asked snidely, turning back to
the magazine.

"I don't think there are age limits on candy," I
said grumpily. "Come on, Lindsay," I said, swinging
the bag in front of her temptingly. "A little sweet-and-
sour fruity treat? You know how much you love
them." I suddenly felt very desperate for Lindsay to
take one. Just one! Just to prove she was the old
Lindsay.

Lindsay quickly scrambled to her knees and
came face-to-face with me.

I smiled. "I knew you'd come around," I said. But
Lindsay looked harsh and serious.

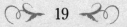

"Cut it out, Haley," she hissed. "Just put the candy away, okay?"

I was shocked. Why was she taking Mackensie's side? Plus, she loved Sour Patch Kids. She always said they were a taste sensation! This was sacrilege!

"I am *this* close to being an official member of the popular group," she whispered, holding her fingers a millimeter apart. "And that means *you* are going to be popular, too." She looked deep into my eyes, and her expression softened. "It's all falling into place. Don't blow it for us."

I sat back in my seat and dug my hand into the bag of candy. I felt a very strange combination of hurt, insulted, and a tiny bit intrigued by the thought of being popular. So far I was not particularly impressed by what I had seen of Mackensie and her followers Taylor, Kaylee, and Brianna up close. But from a distance they were certainly impressive. They set the trends for the class, whether it was what color nail polish to wear or what was the favored snack to pack in your lunch bag. They got invited to everyone's parties. They weren't necessarily the prettiest or the smartest or the most talented or the best-dressed girls in the class, and they certainly weren't the nicest. But they had something that

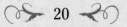

people looked up to. It was a mystery. They thought they were special and everyone else went along with it. I had to admit it was a talent. I wouldn't mind a taste, just to see if I liked it. And if it made Lindsay happy, well, then I'd have to put up with it. Even if I didn't exactly recognize this Sour-Patch-Kids-disdaining, lame-celebrity-gossip-loving girl, I knew underneath was my awesome, funny, practical-joke-loving BFF, Lindsay. I settled into the seat with my candy and my iPod. I cranked up "Race Horse," my new favorite song, and closed my eyes.

"Ugghhhh," I groaned as the bus squealed to a stop hundreds of miles later. I had spent the last hour of the trip reading my book, *Siren's Song*, and absent-mindedly dipping my hand into the bag of candy. The book was gripping, to say the least, and when I looked up, the bag was empty. Now I felt regretful that I was halfway done with the book I had expected to last all trip and slightly nauseous from all the candy I had ingested.

"We're here!" shouted Lindsay's little brother Jack.

I peered out the window and got my first look at the Emerson Inn. It was very rustic looking, like it

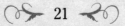

was made out of Lincoln Logs or something. The eaves were strung with red and green Christmas lights, which glowed invitingly, and there was a big wreath with pinecones and a red bow on the door. It looked super cute and cozy. So then why did this shivery unpleasant feeling — almost like dread — snake down my spine? Very weird.

"Isn't it great?" I heard Lindsay say.

"Are you serious?" asked Mackensie. "I thought this was going to be a fancy inn, like maybe with a spa."

I shook off the weird feeling and rolled my eyes. She sounded like such a spoiled princess! I thought about getting up, but the aisle was flooded with McElhinneys, all eager to get off the bus, stretch their legs, and check into the hotel.

Someone sat down on the arm of my chair, jostling me with, well, their butt. I looked up.

"Oh, it's you," Cousin Maddy said, scowling at me over her shoulder. *What's up with her?* I wondered. Then I remembered why she was so cranky. On Thanksgiving I had convinced Lindsay to play a truly inspired practical joke on Maddy. I had found her sunglasses on the kitchen counter and decided we should slip them into the Jell-O mold that Grandma

McElhinney was making. Everyone (except for Maddy, of course) had gotten a huge kick out of passing around the glimmering ring of orange gelatin, with fruit cocktail — and Ray-Bans — suspended inside.

"Please pass the Sunglasses in Aspic!" Grandma had cried, and all the old people had laughed. The rest of us didn't get it.

Well, it was pretty apparent that Maddy was still holding a grudge. Then again, Maddy held a grudge against anyone who'd ever done her wrong. Considering how much she complained about almost everyone in the family, it was amazing she was still coming on these Christmas trips.

When the aisle cleared, I slowly made my way off the bus. The air was cold and I pulled my jacket tightly around me. It was cloudy and the afternoon sun was weak. My breath made big puffy clouds in the air. We all stood around shivering as the bus driver unloaded our bags.

The door to the inn creaked open and we all turned around. A tall old guy with snow-white hair and glasses stood on the porch, wearing a thick cardigan sweater with worn suede patches on the elbows and pants that were baggy at the knees.

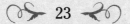

"Hello, McElhinneys and friends of the McElhinneys!" he called. "Welcome to the Emerson Inn. Grab your bags and head right inside. We're a small operation, so I can only check you in one at a time, but there's a roaring fire in the library and we're serving hot cocoa and freshly baked cookies while you wait."

A murmur of appreciation went through the crowd. The innkeeper smiled and held the door open as people trooped in with their bags. He looked to be about the same age as my own grandpa, all crinkly-eyed and grinning. I liked him immediately.

I took a deep breath — still feeling vaguely uneasy — and headed inside. I set down my suitcase in a corner and took a look around. The front desk was strung with silver garland and antique ornaments, and Christmas music was softly playing out of some ancient-looking speakers. I sniffed the air. *Ahhh* — my favorite scent ever — balsam pine. I sniffed again. I could also smell the cookies, and I followed my nose to the library. Shelves crammed with books lined the walls. I was happy to see the familiar yellow spines of my childhood favorites — Nancy Drew. Looked like a complete set. From the fireplace mantel, strewn with evergreen branches, hung four red stockings with white fake fur, belonging to

Elwood, Andrew, Sean, and Harvey. A ten-foot tree stood in the corner next to the window. It was laden with silver icicles, antique ornaments, those funny old lights that bubbled when they got hot, and long strings of popcorn and cranberries. An angel, her hands clasped together, perched on top, her golden halo slightly askew. I looked down at my feet. An adorable French bulldog lay snoring on the carpet, a red bow with the name HARVEY written in cursive lettering on it tied jauntily around his neck. I smiled, my earlier uneasiness forgotten. Sure, there were worn patches on the carpeting, and the floorboards were squeaky. But it was all part of the charm. This was about the most perfect place, short of the North Pole, where you could celebrate Christmas. I picked up a chocolate chip cookie and bit into it. *Mmm* . . . still warm.

Scanning the shelves, I spotted a copy of *The Clue of the Tapping Heels* and grabbed it to show Lindsay. It was the first Nancy Drew book we had read, when we were eight or so, and we had been instantly hooked. We had stopped playing princesses and switched to detectives, taking turns at being the titian-haired sleuth and one of her best friends — George when it was my turn, and Bess when it was Lindsay's.

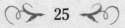

I found Lindsay at the front desk. "Look!" I said, "*The Clue of the Tapping Heels*!"

"Oh," she said vaguely. "Nice." I noticed that she held a room key in her hand. "So, what room are we in?" I asked her. "I call top drawer!"

"Um . . ." Lindsay suddenly couldn't make eye contact with me. "Well . . . um . . . you see . . ." Her voice trailed off.

"What she is trying to tell you," Mackensie explained, "is that she's bunking with me."

I stared at them both. Was Mackensie for real?

"Well, since you know everyone and Mackensie doesn't . . . and, um, think of how great it will be to have your own room!" Lindsay said brightly.

Talk about grasping at straws. "I'm an only child, Lindsay," I said. "I always have my own room."

Lindsay stared into my eyes. Her look said, *Please don't make a big deal out of this. Our popularity is at stake!*

But I couldn't just let this go. I pulled her aside. "I can't believe you're ditching me for her!" I said.

Lindsay looked down at the floor. "Look, I know we had a plan," she said. "But Mackensie asked me to room with her and I didn't know how to say no." She looked into my eyes searchingly. "You understand, don't you?"

I took a deep breath. "I know how important this is to you." I shook my head. "Even though I don't totally understand it."

"I'll make it up to you," Lindsay said, squeezing my arm.

I looked her square in the eye. "I'm counting on it," I told her.

She grinned. "Popularity, here we come."

"I hope it's worth it," I said with a shrug.

"Definitely," she said.

Just then Mackensie barged over and put her arm around Lindsay. "Ready, roomie?" she said. She gave me a grin before they headed upstairs together. A self-satisfied, I-won-and-you-lost grin.

That's when it hit me. Mackensie's best friend wasn't around, so she was going to steal mine.

But why was she being so mean to me? Maybe she was jealous of my friendship with Lindsay. Maybe she didn't think I was fashionable enough to hang out with her. Or maybe she was still holding a grudge against me from that time in third grade when I wiped the floor with her in the class spelling bee.

Whatever the reason, Mackensie was freezing me out. There was no popularity on the horizon for me, that was for sure. My heart sank. This trip was not turning out the way I had envisioned.

Someone walked by and jostled my shoulder. "Sorry, Haley," they said, but I hardly registered who it was. I was surrounded by people, but I felt totally alone.

CHAPTER FOUR

But try as I may, I never can stay upset for too long. After Lindsay and her roomie headed upstairs, I went back to the library for another cookie. I scanned the bookshelves and took note of all the great books on display — *A Wrinkle in Time, Caddie Woodlawn, Charlotte's Web, From the Mixed-up Files of Mrs. Basil E. Frankweiler,* and some of my favorite series — Little House on the Prairie, Pippi Longstocking, Mrs. Piggle-Wiggle, The Boxcar Children, and more. There were stacks of fun games — Clue, Trouble, Yahtzee, Battleship, Scrabble, Sorry!, The Game of Life, and Monopoly, to name a few. And there were a ton of McElhinneys to play them with. All was not lost — I'd make sure to have fun on this trip despite Mackensie's efforts to ruin it.

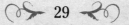

I got my key from the cheerful innkeeper — whose name was Mr. Dowd — and went upstairs. On the first landing I paused to peer at some old-fashioned-looking photos on the wall. A lot of the people in them looked stern and unsmiling, which made me sad and just the tiniest bit creeped out. Were their lives so awful that they had nothing to be happy about? I hoped I never felt like that. Even though things were bad at the moment, and Lindsay was dazzled by Mackensie and company's popularity, I was sure everything was going to turn out okay. She was still the girl I'd known and loved practically my whole life.

By the time I got up to the third floor, I was feeling just fine. I knew my BFF pretty well. I would place a bet that she wasn't going to put up with Queen Bee Mackensie for too long. That girl kept too tight a leash on her group of friends, and Lindsay was a free spirit. It wouldn't be long before Lindsay was her old self again. I just had to be patient.

When I unlocked the door to my room and switched on the light, I was instantly charmed. It was small and cozy and simply adorable, with rosebud-sprigged wallpaper (only peeling a bit), a cute little cast-iron bed, a wooden dresser, and a

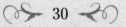

nightstand. I went into the bathroom. The toilet had one of those pull chains — totally old-fashioned. There was even a window seat across from the bed, perfect for curling up with a book or watching the snow fall.

I unpacked my clothes, hung up my ski jacket and pants, and placed my phone, earbuds, and book just so on my bedside table. I put Lindsay's gift in my sock drawer. I arranged my toiletries very nicely on the bathroom counter. (I can't seem to keep my room at home neat, but I love to get organized in hotel rooms!) The lights flickered as I brushed my hair in the bathroom mirror, but I thought nothing of it. I put on my jacket and a hat. Shoving the matching mittens into my pockets, I grabbed the key and went downstairs to see what the girls were up to. I was hoping someone (namely Lindsay) would want to go for a walk to check out Snow City. It would be amazing to spend a couple of minutes alone with my best friend. But realistically, I knew the chances of that were pretty slim.

I took a detour on my way downstairs and checked out the back porch. There was a brand-new hot tub bubbling away. *Sweet.* I'd make sure to return later.

Back inside, I headed for the library. It was empty except for Lindsay's great-uncle Vern, who was snoring on the couch, the newspaper over his face rising and falling with each snore. I giggled. Harvey the dog was still snoring, too, and the two of them were making quite a racket.

"Could our room *be* any smaller?" I grimaced as I heard Mackensie's voice heading down the hallway to the library. "And the dresser drawers stick. So annoying." The girls walked into the library, complaining. They were all wearing their jackets and hats, so I knew my wish for a private walk with Lindsay was not to be.

"I know," said Brianna. "Did you notice that there are two faucets on the bathroom sink? A hot one and a cold one. I mean, no warm water?" She shuddered.

"And there are *wire* hangers in the closet," Kaylee added with a look of horror.

Lindsay stood there, not saying a word.

Uncle Vern broke the silence with a colossal snore.

"Ugh," groaned Mackensie. "Can we just get out of here?"

I stared at the popular girls. *There has got to be something likable about them*, I thought to myself. But I couldn't seem to figure out what it was.

Mr. Dowd walked into the room. He chuckled when he saw Uncle Vern sprawled out on the couch. "Another satisfied guest. Perfect!" he said. He bent to add another log to the fire. "Hello, girls," he said. "Getting settled in? Can I help you with anything?"

"Yeah. Is there anything to do in this town?" Mackensie asked in an obnoxious tone.

I was shocked at her rudeness, but Mr. Dowd appeared to take it in stride. "Why don't you girls explore the shops on Main Street?" he asked. "Don't want you to spoil your appetites before dinner, but Triple Scoop has the very best ice-cream sundaes in town."

"Fine," said Mackensie grumpily. She spun on her heel, and the rest of the girls followed.

I shrugged and took up the rear. "See you later, Mr. Dowd," I said.

"Have fun, girls!" he said.

We walked down the porch steps and set off down the street. Mackensie immediately linked arms with Lindsay, so Kaylee and Brianna did the same.

That left me by myself, a *fifth* wheel. But the scenery was just so lovely — Main Street was quaint, lined with cute houses and shops, their Christmas lights twinkling, their peaked rooftops covered with snow. The shop windows all had inviting displays of the goods they had to offer — jewelry, locally made crafts, brightly colored sweaters, handmade toys.

I was so wrapped up staring into the store windows that I nearly bumped into Kaylee and Brianna, who had come to an abrupt stop on the sidewalk behind Mackensie and Lindsay.

"So, what's going on?" I said. "Want to check out any of the shops?"

Mackensie considered this. "Sure," she said with a shrug. "Pick one," she said to us. The three girls just stood there, apparently unwilling to make a suggestion lest it displease Mackensie. Finally, I broke the silence. "Let's check out this antique store," I said, smiling at Lindsay. Lindsay loved antique stores, flea markets, and garage sales — anyplace where she could sift through someone's old junk. I remembered one time when Lindsay had pored over a wooden box filled with old silver utensils for an hour searching for the perfect spoon to add to her collection. She'd been terribly insulted when the shopkeeper had shaken his head and exclaimed, "My God, it's just a spoon!" Just thinking about it made me laugh.

Mackensie sighed. "Fine, let's go in," she said abruptly. She pushed open the door and we followed her inside the store, Costigan's Curiosities.

As I walked through the door I looked at the display in the window. In the center was a photo of two girls, sisters it looked like, looking sweet and self-conscious in fancy dresses. I stared at it. Something about the girl on the left looked so familiar. . . . I shook my head and went inside.

The store was filled with shelf after dusty shelf of trinkets, dishes, glassware, vases, and frames. In short, lots and lots of old things. From my antique-store experience, I recognized milk glass, Vaseline glass (it glows under black light), and Roseville Pottery. There were old books, posters, lunch boxes, toys, and games. I knew that Lindsay could spend the entire afternoon exploring this place. But she stood in the middle of the store by the cash register, a slightly bored look on her face. It bothered me that she was so determined not to enjoy herself so she could impress Mackensie. But then I shrugged. *Oh, who cares?* I thought. *I can enjoy it enough for the two*

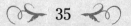

of us. I turned my back on the others and started investigating.

My eye fell on a display case full of dolls, which both totally enthralled me and creeped me out with their staring eyes and slightly open mouths displaying their tiny, perfect teeth. Then I saw it. A Shirley Temple doll in pristine condition, blond ringlets, dimples, and all. Shirley was wearing a white dress with red polka dots and had a pin on her sash with a photo of the real Shirley Temple on it. Now, Lindsay and I had been totally obsessed with Shirley Temple when we were little. We used to rent her movies all the time. My favorite was *A Little Princess* and Lindsay's was *Heidi*. We were so obsessed we asked our moms to sign us up for tap-dancing lessons right after we saw *Bright Eyes*, but it turned out that neither of us was particularly talented at it. Still, we had a lot of fun. I knew better than to call Lindsay over to marvel at my find. That made me feel a little sad.

Mackensie sneezed. "Are you done yet, Haley? I'm highly allergic to dust!"

I wanted to tell them to go ahead, that I would catch up later, but I also had this compulsion to stay with the group. Hanging out with Mackensie might cure me of wanting to be popular for the rest of my life!

"Coming!" I called and headed over to them. But then I spotted a stovepipe hat on a nearby shelf. I stopped and slipped it onto my head. Then — total random bonus — I saw a disguise kit! I opened it up, grabbed a fake beard that hooked over my ears, and walked over to the girls. I thought I saw the corners of Lindsay's mouth twitch. Encouraged, I grabbed the lapels of my jacket and intoned, "Fourscore and seven years ago our fathers brought forth on this continent a new nation, conceived in liberty and dedicated to the proposition that all men are —"

"Can we go now?" Mackensie interrupted. Chastened, I took off the hat and beard and returned them to where they belonged.

The salesgirl gave me a sympathetic smile as I made my way out. "I thought it was funny," she said. "Tough crowd."

"Thanks," I told her. "You have no idea."

Surprisingly, the rest of the afternoon was relatively uneventful. We did some window-shopping, then visited Triple Scoop, an old-fashioned ice-cream parlor with really pretty stained-glass lamps hanging over each table. I got a root-beer float, which was magically delicious. I was tempted to blow the paper off the straw at Lindsay, then thought better of it.

"So, skiing tomorrow!" said Kaylee brightly. "I hope I can make it down the mountain," she said, oozing false modesty. "I haven't skied since Thanksgiving!"

"Me neither," said Brianna.

"I went to Vail a couple of weeks ago," said Mackensie airily.

"How about you, Haley?" asked Kaylee.

I shrugged and took a big sip of my float. "Actually, I haven't been on skis since I was five," I told them. "But you should have seen my snowplow!"

The girls stared. Then Brianna laughed. "Oh, you mean you're a *snowboarder*," she said, nodding.

I shook my head. "No. I mean that I haven't been on a ski slope since I was in kindergarten."

The girls all looked at me like I had three heads. I might as well have announced that I hadn't changed my *underwear* in seven years.

"You didn't tell me that she was a beginner," Mackensie hissed.

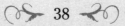

Lindsay jumped in. "Haley's going to be great," she said. "She's so athletic, I'm sure she is going to be a natural."

While I was grateful to Lindsay for having my back, she was stretching the truth. Quite a bit, actually. Me, athletic? I gave Lindsay a funny look. I wasn't sure what she thought she was doing. But she just smiled at me and resumed eating her hot-fudge sundae.

Surely they'd be on to her by tomorrow.

Mackensie muttered something under her breath. I knew she didn't want me to hear her, but it sounded something like "She better not hold us up." But I couldn't be exactly sure, so I chose not to be insulted.

After we paid our bill, we headed up the hill, back to the inn. Mackensie, Brianna, and Kaylee were discussing which outfits they would wear the next day, and I fell into step beside Lindsay.

"Athletic, huh?" I said with a smirk.

"You *are* the best miniature golfer ever," she said.

We grinned at each other. I suddenly felt much, much better about everything.

But it wouldn't last for long.

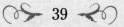

CHAPTER FIVE

On the walk back to the inn, I had a great idea. Correction: I had what *seemed* like a great idea at the time. Lindsay obviously just needed a little reminder of how to be fun again. And the other girls could use a good laugh; they took things way too seriously. One small prank could change the tone of the trip, get it off to a fun start. It was practically my duty to do it.

"Hello, girls," said Mr. Dowd from behind the front desk. "Did you have a good time?"

The other girls mumbled their replies and headed upstairs to change for dinner. I lagged behind them on the stairs. And without warning, I felt a sudden chill in the air as I reached the first landing. I turned to look over my shoulder when —

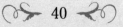

CRASH! One of the framed photos on the wall fell to the ground with a tinkle of broken glass.

That was weird. I picked up the picture and took a look at it. It was a black-and-white photograph of two girls with their arms around each other's shoulders. One girl had braids, uneven bangs, and a smattering of freckles. She was smiling broadly. I could hardly see the other girl's face, as the glass over it had splintered into a million pieces, but I caught a glimpse of wavy, light hair.

I sighed and turned back downstairs, and headed for the front desk.

"I'm so sorry," I told Mr. Dowd. "I guess I must have knocked this down on my way upstairs."

He put down his KenKen puzzle and picked up the picture. "This is such a terrible story. The girl in the picture, the one with the braids, she used to live here at the inn. She died when she was only twelve."

A shiver ran down my spine. "But . . . how?" I asked.

Mr. Dowd shook his head. "I don't really know the details. I just know that she lived here with her aunt and her little brother. And that she got sick and died. Things were different back then. They didn't have all

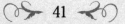

the vaccines that they have today. Kids got the mumps, polio, rheumatic fever, measles. A lot of them got better, but not everyone survived."

Twelve. The same age as me. I stared down at the picture and the girl stared back. She looked so young and so happy. She had no idea that her life would be cut so short so soon. It was devastating to think about.

Changing the subject, I said, "We checked out some shops on Main Street and got some ice cream at Triple Scoop. You were right. It was delicious."

"That's my grandson's favorite spot," Mr. Dowd told me. "Did I tell you that he's coming here for Christmas? Should be here any day now. You're really going to like him."

"That's great!" I said. "How old is he?"

"He's twelve," replied Mr. Dowd. He pulled out a worn brown leather wallet from his pocket and fished out a picture of his grandson. It was one of the most unfortunate-looking class pictures I had ever seen. His grandson looked startled, with wide-open eyes and his mouth partway open, displaying a heavy set of silver braces on his teeth. He also looked like he was about seven.

"Looks like you might need an updated picture," I told him.

Mr. Dowd laughed. "Yeah. I guess you're right. He's grown a bit since then."

"Can I ask you a question?"

"Sure," Mr. Dowd said.

"Do you think it would be okay if I played a little trick on my friends in the library? It would make a small mess, but I would clean it up right after."

"No problem!" he said, not batting an eyelash.

So I asked him for some scrap paper, a hole puncher, and a plastic bucket. Soon my prank was ready. It wasn't a fake-flies-frozen-in-Popsicles-level prank (the one we played last Fourth of July), but it would do.

When I heard Lindsay and the girls coming down the stairs, I ran into the library to set up, and Mr. Dowd told them I was waiting for them. I giggled in anticipation as I heard them approach.

"So it's decided," Mackensie was saying. "I'm going to wear my red ski pants with my black-and-white ski sweater..." The door swung open, the bucket tipped, and homemade confetti rained down on the girls. Most of it landed on Mackensie's head

and shoulders, an unexpected bonus. My eyes flew to Lindsay for her reaction. But my bestie didn't smile at all. Actually, she looked furious.

"What are you, like, an infant?" Mackensie screamed at me, shaking her head so the confetti flew everywhere. She turned to Lindsay. "I can't believe you are actually best friends with someone so immature!"

"Grow up, Haley!" Kaylee sneered.

"It's just confe—" I started to say. But then I stopped. A chill breeze swept through the room and I shivered. It was so cold I could almost see my breath. I looked around for an open window or door. But everything was shut tight.

I was suddenly filled with an overwhelming feeling of dread. You ever hear that expression "A goose walked over my grave"? That's the feeling I had; I felt creepy and weird and shivery. Like something wasn't quite right. Harvey ran in and started barking like crazy. He stopped in front of the window, bared his teeth, and growled.

The girls were spooked. "Did you teach the dog to do that? Are you trying to scare us, too?" Mackensie said to me, her arms tightly crossed.

Mr. Dowd poked his head in the library. "Oh!" he said. "What a draft! I'd better check the windows. Harvey, settle down." He smiled. "Hey, how did your trick go? Funny, huh?" he said to the girls.

"It didn't go over as well as I expected," I told him. "Do you have a DustBuster I can use?"

The dining room had rich wood-paneled walls and two long tables to eat at. Meals were served family style. Tonight we were having fried chicken, mashed potatoes, coleslaw, and buttermilk biscuits. Usually a favorite, but I had kind of lost my appetite after my prank had gone awry.

The girls were all pointedly ignoring me. I knew they were totally overreacting, but I felt really stupid, anyway. I should have listened to Mom — no practical jokes on this trip. I made a mental note to lock the whoopee cushion up in the safe in my room when I went upstairs so I wouldn't be tempted to use it.

There was only one thing to do. "Look," I said to the girls, "I apologize. It was a dumb prank. No more practical jokes. I promise."

Mackensie snorted in a very unladylike way, I felt, and the other girls just shrugged. But Lindsay gave me a grateful smile. My dinner suddenly tasted ten times better, and I polished off two drumsticks and a wing.

After dinner, a bunch of us headed to the library for hot cocoa and games. I settled on the floor in front of the roaring fire beside Harvey and started scratching behind his ears. Mackensie and Brianna played a game of Othello, and Lindsay challenged me to play Connect Four, my favorite. I let her be red even though it has always been my preferred color.

Mr. Dowd came in with a load of firewood, which he added to the big metal ring next to the fireplace. He warmed his hands near the fire and took off his coat.

"So how long have you owned this inn, Mr. Dowd?" asked Lindsay's mom, who sat on an overstuffed love seat, reading a magazine.

"Oh, I'd say about ten years now," he said. "I bought it at an auction for a song." He sat on an ottoman and stretched out his legs. "The story was that this place was haunted. It had been empty for years. No one wanted to buy it."

I shivered, remembering the weird feeling I'd had and the strange chill in the room. And the way Harvey had reacted, barking and growling at nothing

at all. "Do *you* believe this place is haunted?" I asked, leaning forward.

"You sound like my grandson!" he said. "I don't believe in ghosts. Sure, there are some unexplained creaks, but it's an old building. And sometimes I put things down that seem to turn up somewhere else. Then again, I'm old and forgetful!"

"Why does your grandson think it's haunted?" I pressed.

Mr. Dowd smiled. "One night, about three years ago, he woke up and said that his room was so cold he could see his breath, even though the heat was on. And he could make out the shape of a girl, an old-fashioned-looking girl, standing next to his bed, reaching for him. He was so scared he couldn't even move."

I shivered. "That sounds spooky!" I said. "That would certainly freak me out!"

Mr. Dowd laughed. "Oh, it was just a bad dream. And an overactive imagination. Too many chocolate chip cookies before bedtime, I'm sure."

Mackensie snickered under her breath. "He sounds like a loser to me," she whispered loudly.

Brianna and Kaylee laughed, but I did not. A shiver ran down my spine again.

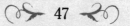

"Your move," said Lindsay.

I inserted a black checker and let it go.

Lindsay's grandpa stood up and walked over to the games shelf. "Hey, you have Scrabble!" he said, spying the worn box. "Anyone want to play a game?"

Lindsay's grandma, who sat knitting on the couch, groaned. "You're so competitive!" she said. "No thanks!"

Mr. Dowd's eyes lit up. "Don't mind if I do!" he said, jumping up. He moved the chessboard off the card table. He and Grandpa McElhinney began to set up.

Lindsay slipped a checker piece into a slot. "I win!" she said. "See? Four in a row!"

I suddenly felt crazy tired. I yawned and rubbed my eyes. "Looks like you did," I said. "I think it's time for bed. Good night, everyone."

Lindsay looked a little guilty, maybe realizing that I had to sleep in a room all by myself. "Good night, Haley," she said. "We're going to have a great day tomorrow. I'll teach you everything you need to know to master the slopes. You'll be a pro in no time!"

"Sounds great!" I said, standing up. "See you at breakfast."

"Good night, Haley!" called various McElhinneys.

I made my way upstairs to my room. When I opened the door, the first thing I noticed was that the lamp on the bedside table was on.

That's weird, I thought. I am a real energy-saving fanatic and always turn off the light when I leave a room. Sometimes accidentally when my mom is still in it.

But I was too tired to think about it. I quickly put on my pajamas, brushed my teeth, and washed my face. Then I shoved my whoopee cushion into the safe. Climbing into the window seat, I made a quick call to my mom to tell her I had arrived safely.

"Are you having a good time?" she asked me worriedly. "Do you have enough socks?"

"Yes," I said. I was having an okay time. And I definitely had enough socks.

We chatted for a while longer, until I could hardly keep my eyes open. A gust of wind rattled the window, and I shivered.

"Good-bye, Mom," I said. "I miss you."

I was asleep as soon as my head hit the pillow. It had been a long day.

CHAPTER SIX

I woke up the next morning to the smell of bacon frying and the feel of warm sunlight streaming through my window. A very pleasant combination. I yawned and stretched and enjoyed lying in the sun for a bit. But the promise of breakfast meats lured me out of bed. I pulled on some sweatpants and a big, comfy sweater and opened my door. I had butterflies in my stomach, a little nervous anticipation, I guess. I was excited to learn how to ski and eager to have some time with Lindsay. She had promised to spend the whole day with me, helping me with my skiing until I got the hang of it. I smiled to myself as I headed downstairs.

"Good morning," I said to Lindsay's grandparents, the only two people at the table.

"Good morning, Haley," Grandma McElhinney said. "Hope you're hungry!"

"You missed an exciting game of Scrabble last night!" said Grandpa McElhinney.

"A real nail-biter," said Grandma McElhinney with a laugh.

"But no worries," said Grandpa McElhinney, ignoring his wife. "We'll have another round tonight!"

Mmmm-mmmm. Since dinner had been so tasty the night before, I had anticipated that breakfast would be good, too. But I wasn't prepared for the feast that had been laid out for us — freshly squeezed juice, piping-hot rolls, and chafing dishes filled with fluffy yellow scrambled eggs, perfectly round pancakes, and crispy slices of bacon. I loaded up my plate with pancakes and bacon and poured warm maple syrup on both. I knew I'd need to fuel up to have enough energy to learn how to ski.

I was munching on a piece of mapley bacon when the rest of Lindsay's family began to make their way downstairs. Lindsay's little brothers were giving me skiing tips (that I didn't understand, though I pretended to) when the girls, all giggling, clattered down the stairs and into the room.

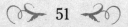

"You totally freaked me out last night, Mackensie!" Brianna said, her eyes wide.

"That was the scariest ghost story ever," added Lindsay.

Mackensie smiled. "I know. I heard it at camp. Imagine having to go to sleep in a tent after hearing that one!"

The girls all squealed with horror.

It seemed that the girls had stayed up late last night telling one another ghost stories by the fireplace after everyone else had gone to bed. They had all been totally freaked out when a book fell off the bookcase in the middle of Brianna's story.

"It fell, just like that!" Brianna said, her eyes wide. "I think this place really is haunted!"

Mackensie shook her head. "Don't be so dumb. You know there's no such thing as ghosts!"

I felt a little left out, even though I was the one who had gone to bed early. I pictured the girls huddled together, taking turns scaring one another as the fire was dying and the flames cast menacing-looking shadows on the walls. It sounded deliciously spooky.

"You know what was really weird?" said Lindsay,

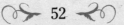

turning to me. "The book that fell? It was *The Clue of the Tapping Heels*!"

That sent a shiver down my spine. "Really?" I asked.

"So, Haley," said Lindsay's dad. "Today's the big day." He began to spoon sugar into his coffee mug. "Are you excited to try skiing again?"

"I am!" I said. "I can't wait for Lindsay to —"

Ptooey! Suddenly, Lindsay's dad spit the brown liquid all over the table.

"Dad! Totally gross!" Olivia exclaimed, wiping drops of coffee from her face with a napkin. She had, most unfortunately, been sitting directly in the line of fire.

"The coffee tastes terrible!" he cried. "What's wrong with it?"

"My coffee tastes fine, honey," said Mrs. McElhinney. She looked puzzled. "What do you think . . ." Then she got a thoughtful look on her face. She dipped her finger into the sugar bowl and took a taste. She made a face. "No wonder your coffee tastes bad," she said with a laugh. "You put salt in it!"

Mr. Dowd, who had been filling Aunt Roberta's coffee cup, came over, looking confused. "That's

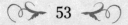

impossible!" he said. "I filled that bowl myself this morning."

Lindsay's mom immediately turned to Lindsay and me. "Girls?" she said questioningly.

I shook my head.

"I don't do that kid stuff anymore!" Lindsay cried, her cheeks flushed with embarrassment.

"But *you* do," said Mackensie, giving me the evil eye.

Lindsay turned to me.

"It wasn't me, I swear," I said. But no one seemed to believe me. I could see how Mackensie, Brianna, and Kaylee might not, considering I had just played a trick on them and all. Plus they didn't know me very well. But Lindsay knew I never lied. Why would I start now?

"Well, I don't know who did it," said Mr. McElhinney in a wounded-sounding voice. "But it was not funny."

He was right. Jokes were only funny when they made people laugh. But nobody was laughing. And Lindsay not believing me? *That* was not funny either.

After breakfast, we agreed to meet back in the lobby in fifteen minutes, ready to head to the mountain. I pulled on my long underwear, wool socks, ski sweater, ski pants, mittens, hat, neck warmer, goggles, and hat. Then I laced up my snow boots and zipped up my jacket. I felt very round and padded, kind of like the Michelin Man. I tucked some tissues, my cell phone, my lip balm, and some money into the zippered pocket of my jacket.

Ready or not, here I come! I said to myself as I headed downstairs.

The girls were all waiting by the front desk for me, rather impatiently, I might add. They all looked so sleek and well coordinated. I was amazed at how expensive their ski outfits looked. Mr. Dowd had dropped off their ski gear — boots, poles, and skis — at the mountain the night before so they wouldn't have to carry the stuff up the hill. I would be renting my gear when we got there.

"See you later, Mr. Dowd," I said as we headed out the door.

He looked at his watch. "Hey, I just got a call from my son. They're almost here. If you wait twenty minutes, my grandson can go with you!" he said.

"Sorry, we've got to run," said Mackensie, pushing open the door hurriedly. When the front door shut behind us, she shook her head. "Honestly. Like we want to hang out with his loser grandson?"

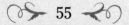

"Did you see that picture Mr. Dowd has of him?" Kaylee added.

Mackensie laughed. "I told Mr. Dowd his grandson was completely adorkable. And I was being really generous."

I felt bad, but I so wanted to spend the day with Lindsay that I didn't even consider waiting for Mr. Dowd's grandson. As we headed to the mountain, I thought I felt the girls all giving me sideways glances. But I wasn't totally sure why. I knew my outfit wasn't as trendy or put together as theirs were, but I didn't think it was *that* bad.

But then when we arrived at the front doors of the ski lodge, I came face-to-face with our reflection. I saw four girls in matching outfits and complementary-colored helmets and gloves. And then there was me. I guess it never occurred to me that cobbling together a ski outfit from borrowed pieces would result in one seriously mismatched ensemble. Purple jacket, green ski pants, yellow hat with red pom-pom, and blue gloves, and none of it fit all that well either. I was one hot, colorful mess. I felt mortified for a moment. But it wasn't like my mom was going to buy me brand-new clothing for something I did once every seven years.

The girls headed off to pick up their skis and poles, and I went downstairs to the ski shop to rent my gear. They gave me an orange helmet. Great — it was the one color of the spectrum I had been missing to fully complete my rainbow outfit. I dropped my regular boots off in a locker, picked up my poles, skis, and ski boots, and started to walk up the stairs.

The rented boots were stiff and hard to walk in, and I immediately dropped one of my poles. I stood there, trying to figure out how in the world — with all the extra padding swathing my body — to bend over and pick it up. Luckily, a passerby handed me my pole. I had so much trouble walking and balancing all of my gear, I had totally broken out into a sweat by the time I got outside.

I spotted the girls standing together. Mackensie, Brianna, and Kaylee were already on their skis, but Lindsay was still putting hers on. As I got there, I marveled as she smartly snapped her boots into the bindings. *Click, click.*

I stood there holding my skis, uncertain as to what to do. Lindsay noticed my distress.

"Put your skis on the ground," she told me gently. I did.

"Now knock the snow off your boots."

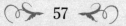

I held on to a nearby ski rack for support as I banged my right boot, then my left, against the other.

"Now slide the toe of your boot into the binding, and stomp with your heel."

The binding clicked up. *One down, one to go.*

"I did it!" I said excitedly.

Mackensie leaned on her ski pole. "What, do you want a medal?" she said. "Yeesh!"

The second boot was not so easy, since I had a large ski strapped to my other foot. I kept losing my balance, and my foot kept slipping out. Finally, I leaned on Lindsay and managed to get my foot in.

"Yay!" I said. I was up on skis and I felt oddly victorious. Which was pretty silly because I hadn't even moved yet.

I watched the girls push off with their poles and begin to gracefully glide to the chairlift. I stared after them. Could I really do that? Um, *how* did you do that?

"Um . . . Lindsay, wait," I called out. I felt a little panicky. Wasn't there a bunny hill I could try first? Did I really have to get on a chairlift right away?

Finally, Lindsay turned around. "Sorry," she said. "I forgot how much of a beginner you are. You just

need to push off a bit, kind of like you're wearing crazy-long ice skates. Come on, you can do it."

I took a deep breath and started sliding my feet one at a time in short bursts. Slowly, very slowly, I made my way to the end of the rope line where the girls were waiting. They did not look happy.

"So glad you could join us," said Mackensie. "Shall we?"

How I made it through the turns of the line without falling on someone I will never know. But I managed it.

We were getting closer to the lift. "Are you sure I should be going on the chairlift right away?" I asked Lindsay.

"Oh, sure!" she said. "We'll go down a beginner slope. You'll be fine."

I gulped.

"What's wrong?" Lindsay asked gently.

"I'm . . . um . . . a little scared to go on the chair-lift," I confessed. "I've never done this before."

"It's a no-brainer," she said. "You slide up to the lifting area. You'll be on my right, so you should put both poles into your left hand and keep an eye on the lift over your right shoulder. As the lift approaches, you should bend your knees and sit

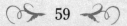

when the seat touches the backs of your legs. You can grab the lift with your right hand as it scoops you up. Then we can lower the bar, and we'll be on our way!"

This was a lot to process. "I put the poles in my . . . which hand?" I asked.

Lindsay's brown eyes were warm with sympathy. She could see that the chairlift really freaked me out. "Don't worry. I'll be with you every step of the way."

We inched our way to the front of the line. When I got closer I got a better look at the lift. It moved faster than I had expected, and my eyes widened with fear.

All too soon we were next in line.

"Whoa! Four at a time," said the lift guy, holding up a gloved hand.

"Oh," said Lindsay. "I totally forgot." She turned to her friends. "Why don't you three go together, and Haley and I will be right behind you."

I held back as Mackensie, Brianna, and Kaylee slid forward. But at the last minute, Mackensie reached over and grabbed Lindsay's arm, dragging my friend along with her.

Lindsay and the girls were scooped up by the lift.

Lindsay turned around in her seat. "Sorry!" she called. "You'll be fine, Haley. I'll see you at the top!"

"Wait!" I called, though I'm not quite sure what I expected her to do. And once again, it seemed I was on my own.

CHAPTER SEVEN

I didn't have a minute to think. Because I needed to move forward, position myself, and get on the chairlift.

"Hurry up," said the operator. I was too slow and a chair went by, empty. I shuffled up to the lifting area. He realized I was scared, took pity on me, and grabbed the chair, steadying it for me. "Sit," he commanded. So I did.

The chair swung back and forth and, suddenly, I was airborne! My legs were dangling and I was afraid of losing a ski. I shoved my poles under my arm, held on to the chair with one hand, and reached up and pulled down the bar with the other. *Whew!* I lifted my feet into place. There, now I had a place to rest my skis. I realized that I would, of course, now have to

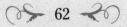

lift the bar before I got off, but it gave me a feeling of security. I noticed that two chairs ahead of me, the other girls hadn't pulled down their bar, daredevils that they were. Lindsay turned around and waved. But I didn't want to let go of my poles or the side of the lift, so I just smiled.

I took a deep breath. Skiers in brightly colored outfits and silly hats were zipping down the hills below. I could see a ski school of tiny little skiers following an instructor and zigzagging their way down across a hill. They didn't even have poles! I took a deep breath. If they could do it, then so could I.

All too soon, the midstation came into view. LIFT BAR, commanded a big yellow sign on a pole. I suddenly remembered that Lindsay hadn't told me how to get *off* this thing. I felt panicked. I switched my poles to the other hand and pulled up the bar. And, suddenly, my skis were touching the ground.

"Stand up!" a voice called out. It was Lindsay. I stood and the lift pushed me a little, giving me the momentum I needed to slide down the incline. Unfortunately, I panicked a bit, snowplowed, and my ski tips crossed. I went down like a sack of potatoes. Can you say *embarrassing*? I spit some snow out of my mouth, then somehow managed to pull myself to

my feet and shuffle over to the girls, completely humiliated.

"Well, that was . . . graceful," said Mackensie. She sighed. "So I assume we're doing Whispering Pines?" she asked. She pronounced the name of the beginner slope like it was some sort of incurable disease.

"Until Haley gets the hang of it," said Lindsay lightly.

There was a beautiful big green circle in front of the name of our trail, I was happy to note. With a toss of her helmeted head, Mackensie took off, not looking back. In spite of myself, I watched her in awe. She was incredibly nimble. So were Kaylee and Brianna. They made it look easy.

But it certainly was not.

It soon became clear that I was not going to win a gold medal in speed or form. As a matter of fact, a tiny boy zipped by me, shouting, "Try to catch me, Grandma!" and was immediately followed by a white-haired old lady. *Speed demons*, I muttered to myself. But Lindsay was patient and kind, coaching me down the hill, reminding me to bend my knees and keep my hips positioned correctly. I had a big, proud grin on my face when we reached the bottom. I think I deserved a bronze medal in Not Falling. Or maybe even a silver.

"Great job!" Lindsay said when we finally reached the bottom. She grinned at me. "I'm really proud of you."

Mackensie, Kaylee, and Brianna did not seem so impressed.

"I didn't come to the best ski mountain in the tristate area to stand around waiting," Mackensie complained.

"Well, Haley and I are going to do that hill again, so why don't you guys do Bear Trap and we can all meet for lunch at twelve thirty?" suggested Lindsay.

Yes! I thought.

Mackensie's eyes narrowed. "Are you sure, Lindsay? Didn't you want me to show you that move I just learned in Vail?"

Lindsay glanced at me. "Maybe we can do it later this afternoon," she said.

Mackensie rolled her eyes and headed off with Kaylee and Brianna. And I had my best friend all to myself for three whole hours!

The lift was much easier with Lindsay by my side, and after a couple of runs, I started to feel a little bit

more comfortable on my skis. I was still snowplowing, but not quite so shakily. And Lindsay and I had the absolute best time. We laughed and reminisced and acted stupid, just like old times. We talked about everything under the sun, with one notable exception — I didn't mention what a colossal witch Mackensie was. It seemed like a topic Lindsay wouldn't really want to discuss.

All too soon it was lunchtime. I didn't want my alone time with Lindsay to come to an end. But my cheeks were cold, and I was starving. Plus my legs were feeling a little shaky from the unfamiliar workout I was giving them. It was definitely time for a break.

The cafeteria was full of people stomping about in their ski boots as they chose their lunches from a large selection of salads, entrées, and sandwiches. I somehow managed to keep my turkey chili, corn bread, and water all on my tray as I clomped back to the table.

We all had worked up pretty big appetites. Everyone munched along companionably in silence.

"So, how did your morning go?" Brianna finally asked.

"It was a lot of fun!" I said.

"Yeah," said Lindsay. "Haley is really getting the hang of it."

"Well, we skied two double black diamonds," said Mackensie. "I'm sorry you had to miss it," she said pointedly to Lindsay. She took one last noisy sip of her diet soda. "Time to hit the slopes, girls," she said. She stood up and looked over her shoulder. "Coming, Lindsay?"

Lindsay stood, then sat back down. She turned to me with a guilty look on her face. "No, I'm going to ski with Haley," she said.

I took a deep breath. "Go," I said, flapping my hand at her like I was shooing away a pigeon. "Do a double black diamond for me!"

The look of relief on Lindsay's face was not surprising. But it didn't make me feel any better. She hurried off to join her friends.

"So," I said aloud. "All by yourself." I was tempted to turn in my skis for the day and go back to the lodge. But something told me not to give up. "Just one more run," I pep-talked myself. "You're starting to get it. Keep going."

After I returned my tray, I headed outside, found my skis, and after two or three tries, got them on my feet and duck-walked to the lift. And this time, I got on, no problem. I was feeling pretty pleased with myself as I lowered the bar. Pretty soon, I made my way to the top of a brand-new beginner hill — Elmira's Gulch. I was getting the hang of skiing, and it felt pretty good.

Look at me, I thought as I slowly made my way down the hill. *I'm skiing all by myself. Maybe by the end of this trip I will be an expert. I'll challenge Mackensie to a race and beat her hands down.* Then I laughed at myself. That was never going to happen, but it was a nice daydream.

As I started to gain a little speed, I did a turn. I even managed to keep my skis a bit parallel, like Lindsay had been trying to teach me. But then disaster struck. I hit an icy patch, lost my balance, and totally went out of control. A little Speedy Gonzales shot around me. *"Ahhhhh!"* I yelled, startled. I twisted to avoid him and . . . *CRASH!* I ran right into the skier passing on my left.

I hit the ground hard and started to slide, bumping on the ground all the way down the hill. *Oof! Ouch! Ow!* I finally came to a stop, my face full of snow.

"Hey, are you okay?" said a voice. When I looked up, I realized it belonged to the skier I had just run into. Embarrassing!

"I'm really sorry," I said, staring up at the sky.

"I'm sure it was totally my fault," he said.

I sighed. "Oh, no. I'm pretty sure it was mine."

"Are you going to lie there all day?" he asked.

"I'm considering it," I replied. I planted my poles in the snow and tried to use them as leverage to lift myself up, but I couldn't seem to get more than a few inches off the ground. "Actually, I, um, can't get up," I admitted.

"Let me give you a hand?" the skier asked. He leaned over, flashing me a gleaming smile. I caught my reflection in his goggles. It was not my most graceful moment, that was for sure.

I was embarrassed and wanted to say no, but I was desperate. So I took his hand and let him pull me to my feet. But just as I was almost upright, I started to slide forward, and yanked his hand . . . pulling him down right on top of me.

"Oof!" I said. Can you say *mortifying*? I'd knocked this guy down *twice*.

"Well, that was unexpected," he said as he rolled into the snow. Then he burst out laughing. After a moment, I joined in.

My laughter was cut short as he removed his goggles to wipe his bright blue eyes. The intensity of

their color perfectly matched the blue ski jacket he wore. After staring for a moment too long, it occurred to me that he was my age — and he was devastatingly cute. We're talking movie-star handsome here. I would definitely have to tell Lindsay about him later.

"Can I give you a tip?" he said.

I nodded.

"When you're trying to get up from a fall, make sure your skis are perpendicular to the slope. Otherwise, you could end up sliding all the way down the mountain. Watch me."

He carefully positioned his skis, planted his ski poles in the snow next to his uphill ski, and hoisted himself up. I could hardly say a word, but tried to copy what he'd done. "Thanks," I whispered when I was on my feet.

"No problem. Good luck!" And with a wave and a dimpled smile, he took off.

Well, at least I won't be seeing him again, I thought. Still, he was so cute it had almost been worth the humiliation.

Once I had collected myself, I set off slowly and deliberately. I was not going to let that happen again, that was for sure.

As I snowplowed to a stop at the bottom of the hill, imagine my surprise when Blue Jacket Boy was waiting for me. "Going back up?" he asked, pointing to the ski lift.

To my even greater surprise, I really wanted to. And not just because he was so cute and I wanted to sit next to him. I actually wanted to ski some more.

"So, what's your name?" he asked when we were sitting side by side on the lift.

"Haley," I said. "What's yours?"

"Sean," he replied. Turned out we were both in the seventh grade. He had been skiing since he could walk. He sometimes raced, but he didn't like snowboarding.

"Well, I'm a beginner," I said. "In case you hadn't already noticed."

I managed to make it off the lift without falling. Score one for me!

"See you later, Sean," I told him, pointing myself in the direction of Winding Way, another green circle slope I thought I would try next.

Sean suddenly looked shy. And it made him look even cuter than ever, I swear. "Um, do you mind if I ski with you?" he asked. "My dad's knee is bothering him, and he can't ski with me on this trip."

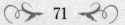

71

Did I mind skiing with the world's cutest boy? Was he kidding?

"Are you sure?" I asked. "I'm pretty slow, you know. And I only do beginner slopes."

"I'm sure," he said. "It's way more fun to ski with a friend. I can do the double black diamonds by myself any day."

Ohhhh. That was sweet. My heart melted a little when he called me his friend. This afternoon was shaping up to be way better than I'd thought. Turns out being abandoned by your best friend can sometimes have an upside. And Sean was an even better teacher than Lindsay. By the end of the afternoon, I was starting to do stem turns, which are halfway between snowplow and parallel turns. I wasn't doing them well, mind you. But I had a feeling my snowplow days were over. We had a great afternoon talking about our schools and clubs and the stuff we were into. He liked to watch baseball, read mysteries, and was a big fan of Agents Scully and Mulder, just like me.

We skied until the slopes were about to close, and I even made it down without falling again — victory! After we turned in our skis, poles, and helmets for overnight storage, we walked outside into the crowd, and I spotted the rest of the girls. "Hey, Lindsay!" I called, waving. "Wait up!"

They all spun around.

"Guys, this is Sean," I said, relishing the shocked looks on their faces when they saw my handsome new friend.

"Sean, this is Lindsay, Kaylee, Brianna, and Mackensie," I said.

"Hey," he said. "Haley and I ran into each other on the slopes today." Our eyes met, and we burst out laughing like we were old friends telling a favorite joke.

Mackensie was confused. "So you guys already know each other?" she asked.

"No," I said. "We literally ran into each other!" Sean and I laughed again.

Mackensie somehow jostled herself in between Sean and me as we headed back to the inn for dinner. She started peppering him with questions: where he lived, what school he went to, what he liked to do for fun. He had hardly answered one question before she started up with another.

"Well, here we are," she said when we reached the front steps of our hotel. "The Emerson Inn. One word of advice — don't stay here."

"Really?" said Sean. He had a bemused look on his face. "How come?"

"It's totally run-down, and the rooms are too small," she explained.

"And the bathroom faucets are weird!" Brianna piped in.

I turned to him. "Don't listen to her. It's really great. It's cozy and cute, and the food is delicious."

"I know," said Sean.

"Well, good-bye," I said as we turned to walk inside. "It was really nice to meet you. I had fun today." But to my surprise, he followed us up the steps.

Mr. Dowd's face lit up as we walked in.

"Hi, Mr. Dow —" I started to say. But Sean interrupted me.

"Hey, Grandpa!" he said.

CHAPTER EIGHT

"But I swear I didn't know who he was!" I protested.

I had changed into my comfiest jeans and an ultrasoft black turtleneck sweater for dinner and was sitting in the library waiting for the dinner bell to ring. As soon as I'd walked into the room, Mackensie had pounced on me. And, boy, was she mad.

"I totally humiliated myself in front of him!" she said. She narrowed her eyes at me. "Another one of your famous practical jokes, I guess?"

I could feel my heart beating faster. I was angry. Mackensie had opened her mouth and inserted her foot all by herself. She didn't need any help from me. No way was she pinning this one on me! I took a deep breath before I spoke to calm myself down.

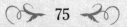

"No, I wouldn't set you up to say mean things about the inn. I don't think that's funny at all. Face it, Mackensie, you said something rude and stupid. And you have no one to blame but yourself." I felt proud of myself for standing up to her without being mean.

"But . . . but . . ." Mackensie spluttered.

Ring-a-ling! Saved by the dinner bell! I turned and headed for the dining room. My stomach was growling and I couldn't wait to eat. I got caught up in a bottleneck of McElhinneys as everyone rushed for the door. I guessed everyone was hungry after a day on the slopes. A hand reached out and touched my shoulder. I turned around and saw that it was Lindsay.

"Hey," I said. "I really didn't know who Sean was. And I didn't switch the salt and sugar today at breakfast," I told her. "I've never lied to you before, and I'm not starting now."

Lindsay smiled and squeezed my hand. "I believe you, Haley."

Relief swept through me. As long as Lindsay believed me, I didn't care what anyone else thought.

When I walked into the dining room, Sean waved to me from one of the tables. "Hey! I saved you a seat!" he called. He was wearing a blue sweatshirt

and it looked like he had washed his hair — it was shiny and soft, and you could still see the comb marks separating his brown locks. I smiled and crossed the room toward him. "Your friends can join us, too, if you want," he said.

I sat next to him and waved over the girls. Mackensie shoved herself past Brianna and into the seat on his other side. "I was totally kidding before," she purred. "This is the best inn, like, ever."

"I totally agree," said Sean, elbowing me in the side. "This is my dad, Andrew Dowd," Sean said, introducing us to a man sitting across the table, who looked like an older version of him. "Dad, this is Haley and . . ." He paused.

"Lindsay, Mackensie, Brianna, and Kaylee," I offered.

"Pleased to meet you all," said Sean's dad. He turned to me. "Are you the Haley that Sean spent the afternoon skiing with?"

I admitted that I was.

"Sean says that you have great potential," his dad said. "He thinks you'll be a real skier by the end of the week."

I could feel my face getting hot. "Really?" I asked Sean.

"Really," Sean replied.

Dinner was totally fun. Sean and his dad made everyone laugh with stories about the inn and a cranky cook who used to work there, who would yell at everyone. There was no talk of practical jokes and no fingers of blame being pointed at anyone. It seemed like things were finally getting back to normal.

After the dinner was eaten, the table was cleared, and the coffee was poured, Mr. Dowd made an announcement. "We have a very special dessert tonight," he said. "Decorate-your-own Christmas cookies!"

"He does this every year," said Sean. "It's really fun."

"I haven't decorated Christmas cookies in years!" cried Mackensie. "Sean, will you help me?"

Sean gave me an is-she-serious look. But he smiled and said, "Sure!"

Mr. Dowd brought out plates of sugar cookies in the shapes of stars, Santas, reindeer, wreaths, and snowmen. There were candy canes, presents with bows, rocking horses, and Christmas trees. Then he brought out pastry bags filled with brilliantly col-ored icing and jars of sprinkles, sugars, and candies. I grinned. This was going to be a lot of fun.

I grabbed a snowflake and Sean a tree. We went straight to work.

"That's a beautiful cookie!" Mackensie exclaimed when Sean was done. I glanced over. He had frosted the tree green, then pressed M&M's into it. He finished it by frosting the star on top in yellow.

"Thanks," he said. "I made it for . . ."

I could see the expectant look on Mackensie's face.

"Haley," he finished, handing it to me.

I could feel myself blushing as I accepted the cookie. "Thanks, Sean," I said and took a big bite. "Delicious."

"I like your snowflake," he said, looking over my handiwork. I had traced a pattern in white icing and sprinkled pink sugar crystals over it.

"Then it's yours!" I told him as I started in on another design.

There was a commotion from across the room. "I hate my cookie!" a little voice yelled. It was Boris — the four-year-old with the temper-tantrum problem.

I had another of my "great ideas." I walked over to him and handed him the cookie I'd been working on. I was pretty proud of it. It was a snowman with red frosting mittens, a blue top hat, and an orange

carrot nose. "Hey, how would you like a snowman cookie?"

"That's so sweet, Haley," cooed Aunt Betsy. A smile stretched tightly across her face. "What do you say when someone does something nice for you, Boris?"

"I hate YOUR cookie, too!" he yelled at me. I was pretty sure this was not the response Aunt Betsy had in mind. Then he picked up my awesome snowman and threw it at me. It hit me in the head.

"Bedtime!" Aunt Betsy said with a sigh. She had to drag him out of the room kicking and screaming. "Sorry, Haley," she called.

"Nice job," said Sean, as I returned to our table, slightly chagrined.

"Shut up," I said teasingly. "Boris was just jealous of my amazing cookie-decorating skills. He knows he can't compete."

"Yes, I'm sure that's it," said Sean drily.

As the evening wore on, we decorated and laughed. A lot. Sean said my polka-dotted rocking horse looked like it had chicken pox, and I mentioned that his Rudolph with the red M&M for a nose looked like he had a bad cold. It was all in good fun, of course. Mackensie looked like she wanted to reach

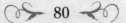

across Sean to throttle me. *Hey* — I realized. *Miss Popularity is jealous. Jealous of little old me.*

As we were decorating the last batch of cookies, Mr. Dowd came out with the evening's hot cocoa on a silver tray. "Why don't I bring the cookies to the library and we can have them with our hot cocoa?" he asked.

"We can't forget to save some for Santa!" six-year-old Cousin Elise said earnestly.

"Of course not," said Mr. Dowd. His face broke into a smile as he walked over to the breakfront, rummaged around inside, and pulled out a colorful plate. He brought it over to our table and showed it to Sean and his dad. "Remember this?" he asked.

Sean looked at the plate and grinned. COOKIES FOR SANTA was written on it in childish printing, and there was a cute kid drawing of Santa eating an insanely ginormous cookie. "I made it with Nana when I was six," he said softly. "I drew the picture on a piece of paper, and then she mailed it away. It came back on a plate. She made the best cookies. . . ." His voice trailed off.

I gathered from the wistful looks on Sean's, his dad's, and his grandpa's faces that Nana was Mr. Dowd's wife and that she was no longer with us.

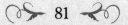

"That is a really nice plate," I said to Sean. "It's so nice that I am going to put the best cookie of the night on it. My snowman with the mittens and scarf, of course."

A smile returned to Sean's face. "Oh, I think you are sadly mistaken!" he said. "You must mean my Santa with the candy buttons on his coat."

Elise gave us both a puzzled look. "Why are you two arguing?" she asked. "There's room for lots of cookies on this plate!"

Once we had put several cookies aside for Santa, we brought the rest to the library. Grandma and Grandpa McElhinney were already there, sitting comfortably in front of the fire. "Yum!" said Lindsay's grandpa, digging right in. As everyone made themselves comfortable on various couches and chairs, I sat on the floor next to Harvey and started scratching behind his ears. He sighed with contentment. Sean flopped down on the braided rag rug next to me.

"Harvey really likes you," he said.

"I have a feeling Harvey likes anyone who scratches him," I replied.

Sean thought for a moment. "Well, you're probably right. But I still think he has a special place in his little doggie heart for you."

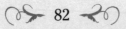 82

"Does anyone need anything?" asked Mr. Dowd. Everyone was munching cookies and sipping hot cocoa. We were all totally, wonderfully fine.

"How about another game of Scrabble?" Grandpa McElhinney called out.

Mr. Dowd's eyes lit up. "You don't have to ask me twice!"

"Grandpa's obsessed," said Sean. "He once got a triple word score on *musquash*, and he hasn't stopped talking about it since."

"Is that even a word?" I asked.

"Apparently it's another word for muskrat," Sean explained.

Mackensie was perusing the game shelf. "Trouble or Battleship?" she called over her shoulder to Sean.

"I am a big Trouble fan," Sean admitted. "But only if I get to be green."

"Trouble it is," said Mackensie, pulling down the box and placing it on the coffee table. Brianna and Kaylee scooted over and started squabbling over who was going to be red.

Mackensie looked over at me. "Oops, only four players," she said with a sly smile.

"That's okay," said Lindsay. "Wanna play Spit?" she asked me.

"Do you even have to ask?" I said. Spit was one of our favorite card games of all time.

"There's a pack of cards in one of the drawers in the front desk," Mr. Dowd called from across the room.

I stood up and walked out to get the cards. A door slammed down the hallway and for the strangest second, I thought I heard the sound of someone crying. But when I poked my head back in the library, everyone looked happy and content. I shrugged, and resumed my search for the cards. I had to pick through various odds and ends in the desk — menus, matches, string, old photos, and safety pins — before I finally found them in one of the drawers.

I returned to the library. "Found them!" I said, holding the cards aloft. When we were all set, I counted. "One . . . two . . . three . . . spit!" There was a flurry of cards as we each tried to get rid of as many as possible.

Mr. Dowd and Grandpa McElhinney started setting up the Scrabble board, trash-talking each other the whole time. "I'm going to wipe the board with you, Dowd," said Grandpa McElhinney with a laugh.

"George, really," Lindsay's grandmother said, not looking up from her magazine.

"Hello, everyone," said a voice. I looked up. It was Aunt Roberta, Lindsay's funny aunt, who was still wearing those ridiculous furry boots. I inched over a bit so she could pass. She plopped herself down in an armchair.

Pfffffffffttttttttttttttt! A crazy-loud — and awesomely rude — sound filled the air. Aunt Roberta's eyes were huge. She looked mortified. "My goodness!" she said.

The little cousins started laughing so loudly they couldn't breathe. Lindsay's brother Sam was literally rolling on the ground. The grown-ups were trying hard to keep straight faces, but they weren't really succeeding. I couldn't even look at Lindsay for fear I would crack up at poor Aunt Roberta.

"Roberta, are you trying to distract me?" asked Grandpa McElhinney. That was it. Uncle Dave could hold it in no longer. He howled with laughter. Everyone else joined in.

"Don't be ridiculous, Dad," Aunt Roberta said huffily. Then she got a funny look on her face and started fishing around on the seat underneath her. "Aha!" she said, brandishing a whoopee cushion in the air. "I don't know who put that underneath me, but it wasn't very funny!" she said.

All eyes flew to Lindsay and me.

"It wasn't us," I protested.

But Lindsay looked at me, anger in her eyes. "How could you?" she said. "Embarrassing Aunt Roberta like that? Grow up, Haley. Enough is enough."

"But I didn't . . ." I started to say. Then I looked at the whoopee cushion, which Aunt Roberta still held in the air.

It looked exactly like the one I'd brought. The one I'd locked in my bedroom safe.

CHAPTER NINE

Lindsay looked at me. "I gave you that whoopee cushion," she said. "You can't deny it."

I shook my head. "I know it *looks* like mine," I said. "But it can't be. Come upstairs; I'll prove it to you."

I quickly made my way upstairs, Lindsay at my heels. Mackensie, Brianna, and Kaylee tagged along behind her. I unlocked my door, my hands shaking a little. I was so mad at being unjustly accused.

I strode over to the closet and punched in my code, my birthday, 0816. The safe made a whirring noise as the door popped open. I turned to look back at the girls as I pulled the door wide. "See," I said. "It couldn't be me."

Mackensie peered inside. "Pathetic," she said. She tossed her hair and left the room, Brianna and Kaylee right behind her.

Huh? I peered into the safe. There was no whoopee cushion. But there *was* a cookie sitting there. A snowman with a jaunty red hat, mittens, and a carrot nose.

I stared at the cookie. "But . . . but . . ."

Lindsay shook her head. "What is wrong with you?" she asked.

"But I didn't do it!" I said. "Someone stole my whoopee cushion and replaced it with my cookie!" Even as I said the words, I knew how ridiculous they sounded.

"Only one person left the room, Haley. I keep standing up for you to Mackensie and you keep doing stupid things!"

"I'd believe you, no matter what," I whispered.

"That's easy for you to say," Lindsay replied. "You might as well have been caught red-handed. You're lying, and you won't admit it."

"Why would I do all of this? It's only making everyone mad at me. It doesn't make sense. And, um, who in their right mind would put a cookie in a safe?"

"Mackensie says you're doing these things for attention. Because you're jealous of our friendship."

"I *am* a little jealous, Lindsay," I said. "You're my best friend, and I'm feeling left out. But not enough to do stupid things to get myself in trouble. It just makes no sense!"

"I'm hanging out with Mackensie for both of us," said Lindsay. "And you're totally ruining it."

"Well, I didn't ask you to do anything for me," I told her.

Lindsay shook her head. "Just stop the practical jokes and everything will be fine. She's not so bad, really. You have to admit she has great taste."

"She's awful, Lindsay. She's mean and selfish. And that's not even the point. You don't get it. I'm *not* pulling those pranks. Ever since the confetti over the door, I haven't done anything."

Lindsay shook her head. "I want to believe you, but I just can't."

"Fine," I said angrily. "Go downstairs and hang out with your new BFF."

Lindsay stuck out her lower lip. She looked exactly like she did when she was four and her mother told her that no, we couldn't give the cat a bath. "Fine, I will."

"Fine," I said again. But I didn't feel fine. I could see both sides of the story. It *did* look like I was guilty. Only, if the situation was reversed, I would have had Lindsay's back no matter what. She was taking sides — but it wasn't my side. I felt an intense mix of emotions. Angry. Sad. Embarrassed.

I sulked for exactly fifteen minutes. Lindsay and I had never fought quite like this before, and I needed to think about what that meant. Plus, somebody was trying to make me look bad. Something weird was definitely going on and I needed to get to the bottom of it. But first I needed a little time to think. So I put on my bathing suit and flip-flops, wrapped my towel around me, and headed for a long soak in the hot tub under the stars. I hoped everyone was still hanging out by the fireplace and I'd have the whole hot tub to myself.

No such luck. I heard voices as I pushed open the back door. My ears pricked up as I distinctly heard my name mentioned. And not in a flattering way. More like in an I-can't-believe-you-are-best-friends-with-such-an-immature-weirdo kind of way. I couldn't tell who was saying it, but it didn't matter, anyway.

I may not have recognized the other voices, but I'd know Lindsay's anywhere. So when I heard her respond, I saw red. "I know, can you believe it? Sooooo immature," she said. How could she? Lindsay gave me that whoopee cushion. Not even that long ago either. I knew she was a big fan of the embarrassingly funny surprise a whoopee cushion could deliver. But she hid it well.

They thought I was playing all these practical jokes? I'd give them a practical joke all right.

I rushed to the hot tub. "Oh my gosh, I just heard that the hot tub tested positive for dihydrogen monoxide!"

Mackensie gave me a look. But Kaylee asked worriedly, "What is di-di-dihelium? Is it dangerous?"

"Well, it's the number one component of acid rain," I said.

"I don't believe you," said Mackensie. But then I saw a tiny glint of worry in her eyes.

"If it gets too hot, it can seriously burn you!" I added.

"I'm getting out!" screeched Brianna, nearly slipping as she scrambled onto the deck. "I was starting to get pruny, anyway."

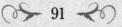

Lindsay gave me a suspicious look as she wrapped her towel around her. She wasn't sure if she should believe me or not, but she wasn't taking any chances. They all headed inside. Once they were safely gone, I climbed in. Ah, bliss! There is something special about being outdoors in the cold air, surrounded by snowdrifts, your breath making big puffs in the air as the stars twinkle overhead. A light snow started to fall, the flakes dissolving from the heat rising from the bubbling water.

When my own fingers started getting pruny, I stepped out, dried off, and wrapped my towel around me. Yikes! It was cold! I shoved my feet into my flip-flops. Just then the back door opened and through the steam I could make out a figure standing there.

"I see you're not worried about the dihydrogen monoxide," a familiar voice said. I blushed. It was Sean. "I hear that it can cause severe burns," he said.

I laughed out loud. "And it's fatal if inhaled," I added.

He shook his head. "There's a sucker born every minute! I have to say I love that you told those girls that the hot tub tested positive for water!"

"Well, water *is* the number one component of acid rain," I said with a straight face.

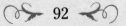

He laughed.

I shivered. "Got to get inside," I said. "I'm freezing!"

"Hey, Haley," he said when I reached the door.

I turned around. "Yes?"

"I have twenty-four-hour access to the kitchen. Do you feel like making sundaes after you get changed?"

That sounded awesome. "Um, yeah!" I said. "I'll run upstairs and put on some sweats. Be down in a jiffy."

I grimaced as I made my way up the stairs. *In a jiffy?* Where had that come from? That was something my grandma would say!

I rubbed my wet hair with the towel, threw on my sweats and a thick pair of socks, and headed downstairs. Not without checking first to see if my whoopee cushion had magically reappeared in the safe. It hadn't. The cookie was still there. I picked it up and tossed it in the trash can. I couldn't even begin to figure out who had put it there and why. As I opened my door to head downstairs, I could have sworn I heard someone laughing in the room behind me. I spun around. But of course, no one was there. That weird feeling came back, uneasy and creepy,

and the hairs on my arms stood on end. *Stop freaking out, Haley*, I told myself. *It's just your imagination playing tricks on you.* I shook it off, took a deep breath, and headed downstairs.

I found Sean in the inn's large, gleaming kitchen. He had set out a row of ice-cream containers on the long stainless-steel island, and brandished a scooper. "We've got Chocolate Chip, Mint Chocolate Chip, Chocolate Chocolate Chip, Heavenly Hash, Rocky Road, Birthday Cake, and of course, Vanilla, Chocolate, and Strawberry," he said.

"What's Heavenly Hash?" I asked.

"Only the greatest ice-cream flavor ever!" he said. "Chocolate ice cream, nuts, marshmallows, and chocolate chips."

That sounded awfully good. "Heavenly Hash it is," I said. Then I reconsidered. "And a scoop of Mint Chocolate Chip, if you don't mind." I could never resist the refreshing flavor — and the awesome color — of Mint Chocolate Chip. Next we moved on to toppings — chocolate sauce, butterscotch, or strawberry. I picked chocolate, my favorite. Then I added nuts, rainbow sprinkles, whipped cream, and a maraschino cherry, of course.

"This is totally awesome," I told him through a mouthful of ice cream.

"Yeah, it's pretty great," he said, putting three maraschino cherries on his sundae.

I looked at him.

"What?" he said. "Who doesn't like maraschino cherries?" He paused. "So, you skiing tomorrow?"

I shrugged. "I guess," I said.

"Want to ski together again?"

"Well, yeah," I replied. "But I'm so much worse than you. . . ."

"I told you, it's way more fun for me to ski slower with someone else than to ski by myself all day," he said.

I didn't want to say it, but I felt I had to. "Mackensie and the other girls are good skiers," I pointed out. "They ski fast. They do double black diamonds. You could go with them."

He shook his head. "You're way more fun than they are," he said. "Plus Mackensie was totally making fun of my grandpa's inn. Why would I want to hang out with someone like that?"

I felt a slow warmth rise to my cheeks. Sean thought I was fun!

Just then a pained look crossed Sean's face. *"Ohhhhh,"* he groaned.

I knew exactly what it was. "Brain freeze?" I asked.

He nodded, hardly able to talk.

"Put your tongue on the roof of your mouth and leave it there for a minute," I said. "It will go away. I swear."

It worked. "Fun *and* smart," he said. "Thanks, Dr. Haley. So," he said. "Can I ask you a personal question?"

I shrugged. "I guess so," I said.

"Where is your family?" he asked. "They don't mind if you're away for the holidays?"

"Well," I said slowly, "I didn't really give them a choice. I kind of wanted to get away from things this year." I took a deep breath. "My parents are splitting up."

Sean nodded sympathetically. "Mine got divorced when I was five. Dividing up the holidays stinks. I do one year with my mom and one year with my dad. Too complicated otherwise."

I nodded.

"So are you glad you came on this trip?" he asked.

"Yeah," I said. "Lindsay's my best friend and I am really close with her family. But . . ."

"... she's trying too hard to impress the blond girl and isn't spending too much time with you," Sean finished.

"That's about it," I said. I looked up from my sundae and smiled. "But I'm still having fun." I looked back down before he could catch me blushing. We finished our sundaes and started cleaning up.

"Well, good night," I said awkwardly when we were through. "Thanks for the make-your-own sundae. See you tomorrow."

"Not if I see you first," he said. Then he grimaced. "Sorry, that was kind of lame."

"Correction — that was *very* lame," I said with a grin. "Have a good night."

I smiled as I walked up the stairs. It had turned out to be a good night after all. And the best part? He hadn't even asked me about the whoopee cushion. He just didn't seem to care.

As I placed the key in the lock, I thought I heard a soft voice whispering my name. "Hello?" I whispered. I peered down the dark hallway and gasped. I could have sworn I saw someone — a kid — dart across the hall. Was one of the little cousins awake and out of his or her room? I headed down the hallway, but it was empty. I suddenly felt spooked, ran back to my

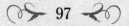

room, and quickly opened the door. I took a furtive look over my shoulder. It felt like someone was watching me.

I closed the door and quickly locked it. *Whew.* I couldn't shake that weird feeling. I took a deep breath and calmed myself down. *It's just all the talk about the inn being haunted*, I told myself as I washed my face, brushed my teeth, and put on my pajamas. *You're psyching yourself out.*

My imagination was playing tricks on me, that was all.

Wasn't it?

CHAPTER TEN

"How about a big glass of dihydrogen monoxide?" Mackensie asked as she shoved a glass at me. Water sloshed over the side, wetting the tablecloth. I hadn't even sat at the table yet. She had obviously been waiting for me to arrive.

I shrugged. "Sorry, guys," I said. "But you have to admit it was kind of funny."

"No, I certainly do not," said Mackensie. "Yet another childish, immature prank."

I sighed and sat down at the table. Just then Sean stumbled in, yawning and rubbing his eyes. He sat down across from me.

"Dihydrogen monoxide!" he said with a grin. "My favorite!"

This time Mackensie laughed. "Hey, Sean," she said. "We took a vote and we decided to do Free Fall today. Wanna join?"

Lindsay did not look happy. "Some vote," I thought I heard her mutter. *Are things going poorly in Popularity Land?* I wondered. *Interesting.*

Sean looked impressed. "That's a tough trail."

"We're all great skiers," said Brianna. Then she looked at me. "Almost all of us."

"Yolo," added Mackensie. She held up her hand, and Brianna and Kaylee each gave her a high five.

I gave Sean a puzzled look. "Yolo?" I repeated.

"You only live once," he whispered. "If I hear that expression one more time, I'm going to throw up." He spoke up. "Actually, I'm skiing with Haley again today. But you might be able to convince me to take one run on Free Fall."

After breakfast we headed to the slopes together. Lindsay was noticeably silent. After we put on our skis and got to the lift, she pulled me aside. "Let's ride up together," she said.

I grinned. I was totally ready to accept her apology for being such an unsupportive friend. Like I said, I roll with the punches.

Once we were safely on the lift, Lindsay pulled down the bar and turned to me. "I'm giving you one last chance to stop it with the jokes," she said.

I shook my head. "I did trick you guys at the hot tub last night, but frankly, I think you all deserved it for being so mean to me. But I had nothing to do with the salt or the whoopee cushion. My old friend Lindsay would have believed me." Actually, I thought, my old friend Lindsay would have planned both those tricks with me. But I wisely left that out.

"It's juvenile and embarrassing. Mackensie says . . ."

"I don't care what Mackensie says!" I yelled. "And the old Lindsay wouldn't have cared either. Now you won't make a peep unless your new best friend Mackensie says it's okay."

Lindsay's mouth fell open. She was mad. "That is so not true!" she said. "I'm still myself. I'm just more . . . popular and you're not, and you can't handle it."

Luckily, it was time to get off the lift before I said anything I might regret. We raised the bar and I carefully positioned my poles so I wouldn't accidentally poke Lindsay in the eye. Not that I wanted to. Well, not really, anyway. Just before we stood I said, "I miss my fun friend Lindsay. New popular Lindsay is a big bore, if you ask me."

And then I skied down the incline and headed to the beginner slope, where Sean was waiting for me. I didn't look back.

And luckily, I didn't fall. That would have totally ruined the satisfaction I felt in getting the last word.

Sean and I had a great time and I began to feel more and more confident on the slopes, progressing to parallel turns. It was a beautiful day, and the sun was strong. I felt awesome as I traversed back and forth down the mountain. I wasn't particularly fast, but I no longer felt like I was out of control. After a couple of runs, I realized I was really thirsty.

"I need a break!" I said when we reached the bottom. "Want to go get some water?"

Sean considered this. "Maybe I'll go try that double diamond run Mackensie was talking about while you get your water."

"Sounds good!" I said. "I'll save Free Fall for tomorrow!"

Sean laughed. "Good idea!"

He headed over to the lift, and I took off my skis by pushing my pole onto the back lever on each ski. I wasn't the most graceful at it, but I didn't fall over into the snow. I leaned my skis and poles against one of the many wooden racks outside the snack bar and stomped inside to get a water.

I sat in the sun and did some people watching. There were tiny kids in brightly colored ski suits zipping down the hill, lots of snowboarders in jeans and sweatshirts shredding down the mountainside, and a whole family wearing matching hats that made them look like they all sported orange-and-green Mohawks. But no Sean. What was taking him so long? Maybe he was having a great time on the expert slopes and had ditched me. I hoped not.

Just then I saw two red-jacketed medics skiing a stretcher down the slope. I wondered who had gotten hurt. Probably some fancy-pants skier doing a trick . . . My eyes widened as I realized that the skier had on a familiar blue jacket. It was Sean!

I stood and crunched my way across the snow as quickly as I could. Which is to say, not quickly at all.

Sean looked embarrassed. "Hey, Haley," he said, waving to me from the stretcher.

"What happened?" I asked. "Are you okay?"

"I totally wiped out on some ice," Sean said sheepishly. "I fell and flew down the mountain face-first." He pointed to his skis lying beside him on the stretcher. "My leg bent so much the binding broke off my ski."

I grimaced. "You didn't — you didn't break anything, did you?"

"No," he said. "I just twisted my knee. I'll be fine."

"Now, stay off the leg for the rest of the day," said the medic as he helped Sean up and onto a nearby bench. "You need lots of ice and lots of rest."

"I can call my dad to help me back to the inn," said Sean.

"Don't be silly," I said. "I'll help you back."

"I don't want to take you away from the slopes," said Sean.

I laughed. "This is a great excuse to call it a day. I'm cold and kind of tired."

Just then Mackensie came barreling down the hill. She came to a fast stop, spraying all of us, Sean included, with snow. I wiped my face with my glove.

"What happened?" she exclaimed.

Lindsay, Brianna, and Kaylee skied over, a little more cautiously.

"Sean twisted his knee," I explained. "He'll be fine."

"What can I do to help?" Mackensie asked.

"No worries," said Sean, sitting up. "Haley's got it covered."

"Oh, I'm sure she does," Mackensie said, pursing her lips.

The girls sat with Sean while I put both pairs of skis and poles into overnight storage. Sean's dad would come back later to bring his skis to the repair shop. Then we said good-bye and headed back to the inn, Sean leaning on my shoulder for support. It was slow going.

Once we arrived, Mr. Dowd helped Sean to his room to ice his knee. I was just in time for lunch, which I ate alone. Everyone else was out skiing or sightseeing. It was quiet and a little lonely.

Then I headed to the library. It was the first time I had the comfy couch right in front of the fireplace to myself, so I grabbed a soft throw blanket and stretched out full-length. With Harvey by my side snoring away, I soon drifted off myself. But it wasn't a peaceful sleep. I tossed and turned, my dreams filled with strange, fleeting shadows.

I woke with a start. I had the distinct impression that someone had been standing over me. The room was getting dark and there was an odd chill in the

air. I must have been asleep for a while. I peered into the gloom. "Who's there?" I croaked. Harvey was gone and the fire had burned down to a few embers. Then I heard a floorboard squeak.

"Who — who's there?" I repeated in a quavery voice. "Hello?"

I sat up, looking all around me wildly. I shivered and clutched the blanket tightly around myself. Then I sat up and switched on the table lamp. I didn't see a soul. I felt foolish. But I couldn't shake the feeling that someone *had* been there, peering down at me as I slept. Suddenly, this overwhelming feeling of sadness overtook me. It almost took my breath away.

I swung my feet to the floor, feeling woozy.

"Hey, check me out," said a voice from the doorway. "Look what Grandpa found in the attic!" Sean stood in the doorway, on crutches. He lifted one and waved it at me.

I blinked at him, still feeling weird.

"Hey, Sean," I said, my voice thick with sleep. "You think this place is haunted, right?"

A cloud passed over Sean's normally sunny face. "You too?" he spat out. "Mackensie was teasing me about that on the chairlift this morning. She thought she was being funny, but I can tell she and the other

girls all think I'm crazy." He spun around as quickly as a boy on borrowed crutches could.

"Thanks a lot," he said over his shoulder. "I thought you were different."

And before I could even start to explain, he was gone.

CHAPTER ELEVEN

Dinner that night was not very much fun. Neither Sean nor Lindsay had saved me a seat so I ate dinner between Will, a somewhat nerdy ten-year-old cousin who was obsessed with the Spanish-American War, and Great-Uncle Lou, who needed a hearing aid but refused to admit it. By the end of dinner I was irritable and exhausted. The evening's conversation had gone something like this:

"How interesting! I had no idea that the Treaty of Paris officially ended the Spanish-American War."

And "Speak up? I SAID, ARE YOU HAVING A NICE VACATION, UNCLE LOU?"

I went to bed early that night feeling sad and homesick. My mom had left me a voice mail asking me how the trip was going. I knew that if I heard her

voice I might start to cry, and then she would insist on getting in the car and coming to get me. So I took the easy way out and texted her back: Sorry, couldn't call, been so busy! Getting much better at skiing. Miss you ♥ H. I felt terrible that Sean thought I'd been making fun of him. And now I was being a big baby by ignoring him back. I would have to apologize to him as soon as possible — if he would talk to me, that is.

"There's no such thing as ghosts!" I said out loud. The bedside lamp flickered on and off several times. Even though I knew I was being silly (an old house with faulty wiring was the only explanation), and even though I hated to waste the electricity, I left the light on that night.

But after a good night's sleep I woke up the next morning feeling much better. Tonight was Christmas Eve. No way was I going to feel sad on my second-favorite day of the year. So what if both Lindsay and Sean were mad at me? Things would work themselves out, they always did. Tomorrow was my *actual* favorite day of the year and there were so many fun things planned — the Secret Santa gift exchange, Christmas caroling in the town square, sledding on the big hill behind the inn, a snowman-building

contest, and a big turkey dinner. I had the world's best gift for Lindsay, and I could hardly wait to give it to her. Even though she would not be winning any friendship medals on this trip, she was still my best friend. I hoped she would see how silly she was being and that Sean would realize I hadn't been making fun of him and we would all be friends again in time for Christmas morning.

I reached for my phone to check the time and knocked over a full glass of water sitting on my bedside table. I had no memory of putting it there the night before. *Man, I must have been really tired last night*, I thought as I got dressed.

By the time I got to the breakfast room it was pretty empty. I filled my plate with pancakes and bacon and dug in as I tried to decide if I would head to the slopes and spring for a skiing lesson with the travel money my mom had given me or maybe go into town and walk around. "Haley!" said a voice. It was Lindsay's mom. "What are you doing here? You should head to the mountain and catch up with the girls!"

"Thanks, Mrs. McElhinney," I said. I didn't bother explaining that I had no desire to catch up with them at all.

She must have seen the sad look in my eyes, because she put her hand on my shoulder. "I have a great idea," she said. "Why don't you take the day off from skiing and spend the day with me? A bunch of us are going to go for a sleigh ride, out for lunch, and then go ice-skating."

I smiled. That actually sounded amazing. "I couldn't think of a better way to spend Christmas Eve," I told her. "I just need to run and grab my jacket."

"Meet us back here in the lobby in fifteen minutes," she told me.

As I headed back upstairs, I decided I would take Lindsay's gift and put it under the tree in anticipation for tomorrow's exchange.

But when I got to my room and opened my sock drawer, I couldn't find it. Had I put it into a different drawer by mistake? I rummaged through them all one by one. No gift. Feeling frustrated, I pulled open the nightstand drawer. And there it was. *I know I didn't put the gift in there*, I thought. I was starting to freak out. Either I was losing it or someone was trying to drive me crazy. I didn't like either option.

I grabbed the gift and my jacket, bounced down the stairs, and placed Lindsay's present under the

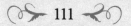

tree, placing it on the patchwork tree skirt, toward the back. And then I took a deep breath and decided to put all my worries out of my mind. I thought it would be easier said than done, but it wasn't. Christmas Eve day was wonderful. When the McElhinneys and I walked down the inn steps, there were two horse-drawn sleighs waiting for us! We piled inside, squeezing together as we nestled under thick wool blankets. The bells on the horses' harnesses jangled merrily as we trotted along. Aunt Roberta (who seemed to have completely forgotten about the whoopee cushion incident, thank goodness) started singing "Jingle Bells," and everyone joined in, the voices from the two sleighs combining together as we went. People waved to us from the street, shouting, "Merry Christmas!" After a delicious lunch and a few hours of ice-skating (another winter sport I am not naturally talented at, I discovered as I spent a lot of time falling flat on my butt) we headed back to the inn in the sleighs. We sang all the way home.

I went upstairs, showered, and changed into a dark green velvet dress with a dropped waist for dinner. Just my style — cute and comfortable. When I walked into the dining room, I gasped. The lights were dimmed and the centerpieces — several large pillar candles surrounded by holly leaves with bright red berries — gave off a warm glow. The table had been set with fine china, sparkling crystal, and actual silver silverware. The dining-room chairs were covered in red velvet, a big gold bow around each one. It was so fun and festive. Curiously, there were colorfully decorated tubes near each plate.

I saw Sean chatting with his dad. I wanted to talk to him, but I needed to get him alone. I didn't think he'd appreciate an apology in front of his father.

Lindsay and the girls sat at the other end of the table. I suddenly felt very awkward. There were only two empty seats — one next to Brianna and one next to Uncle Lou. And the thought of yelling myself hoarse all night gave me the courage to plop down in the seat next to Brianna.

"Merry Christmas Eve," I told them. "How was your day on the slopes?"

They started chatting away, and everyone was actually quite pleasant. I told them about the sleigh ride and ice-skating.

"That sounds really nice," Lindsay said.

"It was," I said. "Your family is a lot of fun."

Clink, clink, clink. I looked up to see Mr. Dowd hitting the side of a crystal water glass with his fork.

"Attention, everyone," he said. "I just wanted to wish you all a merry Christmas Eve and thank you for choosing to spend the holidays with me and my family at the Emerson Inn. Beside your plate you will see a brightly wrapped paper tube. It's called a Christmas cracker, and it is a Dowd family tradition passed down by my father's Irish parents. Have a friend help you pull open the cracker, and see what's inside!"

Brianna turned to me, holding one end of her cracker. I pulled the other end, and it opened with a satisfying *pop*. Inside Brianna found a bright yellow paper crown, a tiny kaleidoscope, and a small folded piece of paper.

"Cool!" she said, placing the crown on her head. She unfolded the paper. "Why does Santa Claus have three gardens?" she asked.

I shrugged. "I don't know. Why *does* Santa Claus have three gardens?"

"So he can hoe, hoe, hoe!" she read.

We all groaned.

Pop! Pop! Pop! People were opening crackers all around us, placing brightly colored crowns on their heads, examining their small prizes — a set of teeny-tiny playing cards, a small bottle of bubbles, an itsy-bitsy magnifying glass.

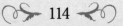

"What is black and white and red all over? A penguin with diaper rash!"

"What happens to Santa if he gets stuck in your chimney? He gets Claus-trophobia!"

"What is green, covered in garland, and goes 'ribbit, ribbit'? Mistletoad!"

I scored a bright pink crown, which I thought was a nice contrast to my green dress. My prize was a key chain shaped like a penguin. Very cute.

I unfolded my joke and read it: "What do you get if you eat Christmas decorations?"

"Speak up!" Uncle Lou shouted.

"I SAID, WHAT DO YOU GET IF YOU EAT CHRISTMAS DECORATIONS?"

No one could guess.

"TINSILITIS!" I said. That one definitely cracked me up.

I looked around the room and grinned at everyone wearing their brightly colored paper crowns. It looked so silly and so festive at the same time. In fact, everyone was wearing one but Mackensie, who didn't want to mess up her hair.

Mr. Dowd stood again. He held his hand over his heart. "My mother, may she rest in peace, was named Antoinette Ciancarelli. And every Christmas

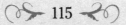

Eve she would prepare the Italian tradition of the Feast of Seven Fishes. To honor her and the other side of my family, we still continue to serve this meal."

My mouth began to water. I am a huge seafood fan. I couldn't believe the amazing food that started to come out of the kitchen. A delicate seafood salad dressed in olive oil and lemon. Baked stuffed clams. Crispy fried calamari. Mussels marinara. Linguine with clam sauce. Lobster. And deep-fried whiting. It was all amazingly delicious. Then came the tiramisu — a delicious combination of ladyfingers, custard, and whipped cream. Yum!

Our bellies full and our colorful crowns still perched on our heads, we made our way to the library to digest our feast.

Most of us just relaxed on various chairs and sofas, too content to move. But the Scrabble-heads started another game. They played for a while in near silence.

Then Mr. Dowd must have taken too long to build his word.

"Here's a twelve-point word for you," Grandpa McElhinney said. "Stumped!"

Lindsay's grandma slammed her book shut. "That's enough!" she cried. "Come on, old man. It's Christmas Eve, and it's time for bed."

Grandpa McElhinney sighed. "Fine," he said. "We'll finish this game tomorrow. Everyone, remember to put your Secret Santa gifts under the tree before bed."

Elise set out the cookies for Santa, a glass of milk, and carrots for the reindeer.

I yawned and stretched. "I'm heading up, too," I said.

Lindsay turned to me. "Merry Christmas! See you tomorrow."

"Merry Christmas, Lindsay!" I said. I could hardly wait for her to open her gift from me the next morning.

Maybe after that, things between us would go back to normal.

CHAPTER TWELVE

As soon as I opened my eyes the next morning, I reached for the phone to call my mom.

"Merry Christmas, Haley," my mom croaked. I had obviously woken her up, as intended.

"Merry Christmas, Mom!" I cried.

Mom laughed. "I thought I was off the hook this year with your pre-sunrise Christmas greeting," she said. I could picture her lying in bed, her hand over her eyes. It's a family joke that I can't wake up early any day of the year except for Christmas Day.

"No such luck," I said.

"I miss you so much, sweetheart," she said. "Are you having fun?"

"Yeah!" I said brightly. "I had a great day yesterday." I started to describe all the new skiing moves

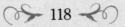

I'd learned and the fun time I'd had with the McElhinneys, then the Christmas crackers and the seven courses of fish.

"It sounds like you're having an amazing time," she said. "Are you and Lindsay having fun? Do you like having a roommate, or do you miss having your own room?"

I didn't want Mom to worry and I knew she would if she found out that I was bunking alone. So I changed the subject. "We're having a snowman-building contest today!" I said.

"Nice," said Mom. "Is Lindsay up? Can I wish her a merry Christmas?"

I thought fast. "She's not here right now," I said. Hey, not a lie, right? "Go back to sleep," I said. "I'll call later to say hello to Gran and Gramps."

"Okay, honey," she said. "Merry Christmas. And don't forget to call your father."

So I did that, too, and had pretty much the same conversation with him. But as I hung up the phone, it finally sank in that we weren't ever going to be spending Christmas as one big happy family again. *Ugh.* I needed to cheer up. It was Christmas, after all!

When delicious breakfast smells wafted up the stairs, I headed down to the dining room. I thought it

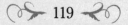

would be fun to eat Christmas breakfast in my pajamas.

Mackensie did not agree. "Are you kidding me?" she said when she saw me in my special Christmas pj's with the candy canes on them.

I ignored her. "Merry Christmas," I said, and went to get myself a glass of juice. But when I looked around the room, I realized that I was the only one over the age of six who was still in her pajamas. Still, I was supercomfy and feeling supremely lazy. In my house we didn't take off our pj's until it was time to eat Christmas dinner. I didn't see why I had to change tradition just because I wasn't at home.

After breakfast I gave in and went upstairs to change. By the time I got back downstairs, the moment we had all been waiting for arrived. We all filed into the library for the Secret Santa gift exchange.

"*Brrr!*" said Aunt Molly, shivering. The room was freezing cold.

Mr. Dowd checked the thermostat. "That's odd," he said. "Maybe this will help." He knelt down and began laying some wood for a fire. Soon it was blazing away.

"Well, if you're all settled," he said, "I'm going to

go open gifts with my family!" He left to join Sean and his dad.

I had heard about the McElhinney Secret Santa gift exchange, but had never participated. It worked like this — at Thanksgiving, each person wrote their name on a piece of paper and put it into Grandpa McElhinney's fedora, then pulled out a name. Everyone bought a present for the person whose name they pulled. On Christmas morning, the person would open their gift, then the fun would begin as they tried to guess who had bought it for them. Grandma McElhinney sat next to the tree, and was in charge of distributing the gifts.

She picked up the first one, a medium-size flat package. "For Boris," she read. "Love, Your Secret Santa."

The four-year-old squealed with delight and ran up to collect his gift. He tore open the wrapping, ripped off the box top, and dumped the contents on the floor in his excitement.

"It's a . . ." He picked it up, then frowned. "What is it?" His lower lip began to tremble.

"It's a flannel nightgown," said his mom, holding it up. "Extra-large. Who is it from? Is this a joke?"

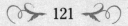 121

"I hate Christmas!" Boris cried.

Aunt Lizzie spoke up. "Um, that was supposed to be for you, Roberta," she said. "Merry Christmas."

Aunt Roberta looked embarrassed and a little mad. "But I don't wear an extra-large!" she said huffily.

Mackensie snorted. "I thought you said this Secret Santa thing was fun," she said to Lindsay. "This is just weird."

"Don't worry," said Grandma. "The tags must have been switched." She picked up another box, a rectangular one. "See, it says *Aunt Roberta* on it," she said to Boris. "So it must be yours." She handed it to him.

He ripped open the box with a little less gusto than before. His lower lip began to tremble. "It's a stupid Barbie doll!" he said. He tossed it to the floor.

Elise screamed, "But *I* wanted a Barbie! Why did Boris get one instead of me?" She burst into tears, too.

Grandpa McElhinney retrieved the Barbie and handed it to Elise. This brought on a fresh round of tears. "I didn't even get to open it!" she wailed.

"What's going on?" her mother asked angrily.

Grandma McElhinney breathed a deep sigh and continued distributing the rest of the gifts. Grandpa McElhinney got a dump truck, which he handed to Boris. Aunt Lizzie got a Justin Bieber boxed set meant for a thirteen-year-old niece. Lindsay's dad got a pink sparkly tutu.

Grandma McElhinney's face was grim. "Haley," she read. She grinned ruefully. "Maybe you'll get a hot-water bottle," she said drily. "Or a onesie."

I laughed and opened the gift. Then I blinked in surprise. It was a copy of *The Wolves of Willoughby Chase*, my favorite book of all time. I opened the front cover and gasped. It was signed by the author, Joan Aiken, herself!

"It's for you, Haley," said Lindsay's mom. "I know how much you love that book."

"Thank you," I said, running my fingers over the familiar red, black, and white cover. Sylvia and Bonnie stood on a snowy hilltop while a snarling pack of wolves circled below. "It's amazing."

"And next is —"

"Wait a minute," interrupted Mackensie. "Don't you think it's weird that the only person so far who got the right gift is Haley?"

"It's just a coincidence," I said. But I noticed that people started looking at me funny.

It was the very next gift that pushed things over the edge.

"Sam," said Grandma, holding up a smallish flat gift. Lindsay's little brother Sam walked over to claim it. He tore open the wrapping, opened the box, then broke out into a big grin.

Whew, I thought. *I'm not the only one who got their own gift.*

"I don't know who this is meant to be for, but I'm keeping it!" he said. He held his gift aloft — a framed photo of the popular girls. There were large, fancy handlebar mustaches drawn beneath everyone's noses.

His twin brother, Jack, gave him a high five. "Classic!" he said.

Mackensie stared daggers at me. "That was supposed to be for Brianna," she said between clenched teeth. "Minus the mustaches, of course."

"Merry Christmas, everyone," said Lindsay's big sister, Olivia, sullenly. "I mean, what a letdown."

Just then the Dowds walked back in, grinning. Mr. Dowd was admiring his handsome new wallet. Sean's dad had a new hardcover book tucked under his arm, and Sean had a cool pair of Skullcandy head-phones around his neck. "Hope your gift exchange was as much fun as ours," he said cheerily.

"No such luck," said Aunt Roberta.

"Oh," said Mr. Dowd, confused. "Hey, George, would you like to finish our game of . . ." His voice trailed off. He was staring at last night's half-played Scrabble board, which had been left on the chess table. His mouth was open in shock. He snapped it shut. "I . . . well, my goodness, this is odd," he said.

We all crowded around. I couldn't see anything in the sea of McElhinneys. Someone gasped and a couple of people gave me funny looks.

"What?" I said. Finally, the crowd parted and I slipped through and took a look. Almost all of the Scrabble tiles had been pushed to one side.

There was a three-word message written in the remaining tiles: HELP ME HALEY.

I backed away, scared.

Lindsay turned to me, her face like stone. "Enough!" she cried. "I'm sick of your stupid tricks! I can't believe how selfish you are! You ruined Christmas! I wish I'd never invited you!"

"But I . . . I . . ." I didn't know what to say. Everyone, even dear Mr. Dowd, was staring at me. I turned to Lindsay's mom. But she was shaking her head at me.

I opened my mouth to speak. But there was nothing left to say. Something truly terrifying was going on and no one believed me. I turned and ran upstairs.

CHAPTER THIRTEEN

When I opened my door, I gasped in shock. I stared at my room, my heart beating fast. It was a disaster area. My neatly made bed was stripped down to the mattress, the sheets, pillows, and blanket tossed on the floor. The drawers had been yanked out of the dresser and clothes had been flung everywhere.

There was a knock at the door. "Is everything okay?" a voice asked. It was Sean.

I opened the door, wide enough so he could see inside. "What do you think?" I asked him.

Sean took one look at the room behind me. "Either you are completely crazy, or there's a ghost in the inn," he said. "I'm going to go with the ghost."

I felt so relieved I almost started crying.

He looked deadly serious. "I guess I know why you were asking me about ghosts the other day. I assumed you were making fun of me. But . . ."

"I wasn't. Weird things keep happening, and I'm getting all the blame. I just thought maybe you'd know something that might help me. Like if there really is a ghost haunting this place, and pulling these tricks, then maybe everyone wouldn't be so mad at me."

"I totally understand," he said. "And I am going to help you get to the bottom of this."

A feeling of relief and gratitude washed over me. I was a little terrified, too. "Why do you think the ghost is picking on me?" I asked. "Doing things so I'll get blamed for them? Sending me messages and tearing up my room like this?"

Sean took a deep breath. "I think she may be a restless spirit who identifies with you somehow. She obviously thinks you can help, right?"

"Help with what?" I asked.

"We have to figure that out," Sean explained. "Then maybe the ghost will be able to find peace and will leave you alone."

"You know a lot about ghosts," I said.

"After I thought I saw her that night, I read a lot of books on the subject," he said. "But I have to say, your experiences have been way more intense than mine."

"Lucky me," I muttered.

"Listen, Grandpa told me that there are a bunch of boxes in the attic that are full of stuff left behind by the previous owners of the inn. We could go up there and see if we can find out any information that might help us."

I nodded. "Sounds like a plan," I said.

We headed to the top floor. There were two unused rooms on either side of the landing, and inside one of them there was a small doorway that led to the attic. Sean opened the door with a *creak* and switched on the light. A small, weak bulb illuminated the room. We saw dusty box after dusty box. There was a huge spiderweb in the corner. I tried not to think too hard about the size of the spider it took to create something that big.

"Where do we start?" I asked.

"Anywhere," said Sean, opening a box.

We found boxes of old taxes, deeds, and other boring paperwork. A box full of dusty law books. An

impressive stamp collection, which Sean put to the side to show his grandfather. Moth-eaten sweaters and old leather shoes that had hardened into almost unrecognizable shapes.

We were getting very grimy.

"Achoo!" I sneezed.

Finally, I opened a box and pulled out a red dress with a white Peter Pan collar that looked about my size. "Now we're getting somewhere," I said. I pulled out more clothes, shoes, some report cards. "Virginia would do much better if she would only apply herself," I read before Sean snatched them away from me. "Stay focused!" he said.

Then I struck pay dirt. A small book with a cracked leather binding. On the front it read *My Memory Book*. I opened the cover. On the inside it said: *Property of Virginia Emerson. Keep Out! This Means You!*

"I think I found something!" I said.

I turned the page. There was a picture of a familiar-looking girl with uneven bangs and braids. It was the same girl whose picture had fallen off the wall!

I flipped through a couple more pages, Sean staring over my shoulder. I could tell he practically wanted to tear the book out of my hands so he could take a

look. There were tons of old photos. Virginia and her dog. Virginia and her little brother. Virginia blowing out the candles on her birthday cake. I turned the page.

"That's weird," said Sean. It was a class picture, Grade 7, with rows of scrubbed, smiling faces in their class-picture best. But one girl's face was scribbled out with pencil so hard it had torn through the paper.

I ran my finger over the list of names below the picture. "That must be Eleanor Thomas," I said.

And that's when the lights went out.

CHAPTER FOURTEEN

Have you ever been in a windowless room when the lights cut out? We're talking complete and total darkness. Like you're at the bottom of the ocean or something. It's terrifying. That's when you can suddenly hear all those awful things that you can tune out when the lights are on — like creaking floorboards, the whistling wind, and the sound of tiny feet scrabbling around in the walls. It made my hair stand on end.

Luckily, Sean had brought a flashlight. Unluckily, it was a miniature one and provided only a minimal amount of light.

Apparently, Sean was not as scared as I was. He held the flashlight under his chin, which gave his face a ghastly glow.

"You're freaking me out," I said, clutching the scrapbook to my chest. "Let's get out of here!"

We hauled the box downstairs to an empty sitting room behind the front desk. I sat on the floor and began pulling cobwebs out of my hair.

Suddenly, the lights flickered back on.

Mr. Dowd poked his head into the room. "I can't figure it out," he said, shaking his head. "We just had the wiring checked last month. Everything should be working fine. And the weather isn't bad enough for a power outage."

Sean and I nodded. We both knew who'd messed with the lights. There was an extra guest staying at the Emerson Inn along with the Dowds and the McElhinneys. And she wasn't happy. Not happy at all.

So instead of caroling at the town square, or entering the snowman-building contest, Sean and I spent the rest of the day going through the old box. We sifted through photos, letters, and drawings, looking for clues about what had happened between Virginia and Eleanor. We found secret notes, birthday cards, handwritten stories starring the two girls, and lots of drawings of a blond girl and a brown-haired girl, all indications of a strong friendship.

Why Virginia was mad — so mad she shattered the glass over Eleanor's face in that picture — was not clear to us. We even found the yellowed newspaper clipping that was Virginia's obituary.

"Look," said Sean, pointing. I looked down. The date of her death was December 25, 1952. It was the exact anniversary of Virginia's death. It was almost too much to think about.

But we were not any closer to solving the mystery and putting this spirit to rest.

And I couldn't help wondering. What would Virginia do next?

Sean and I barely made it through Christmas dinner. We couldn't eat a thing, which was a shame as it was a delicious-looking turkey with all the trimmings. Exhausted, we each snuck off to our own bedroom before dessert.

I brushed my teeth sleepily, rinsed, and spit. Then I straightened up and glanced in the mirror.

I gasped. There was the outline of a face in the mirror over my shoulder. I tried to scream, but no sound came out. My eyes bugged out of my head as I took in the uneven bangs, the pale face.

It was Virginia Emerson. And she did not look happy at all.

But when I spun around, no one was there. I shook my head in disbelief. Had I really just seen a ghost?

"Virginia?" I said when I finally could speak. "We're trying to help you."

I thought I could hear the faint sound of crying. But I wasn't totally sure.

So I kept the light on again that night. And I didn't sleep well at all. I lay completely still, terrified that ghostly hands were going to grab me in the middle of the night, begging me for help. Every *creak*, every tiny sound, had me petrified with fear. I was completely relieved when the sun finally came up. Things always seem less spooky in the clear light of day.

Sean had big dark circles under his eyes the next morning, too. We sat together at the breakfast table flipping through Virginia's scrapbook, hoping to find a clue we might have missed yesterday.

"I just don't get it," I muttered. "They did everything together. They were as close as sisters. Why is Virginia so unhappy?"

"Do we have it all wrong?" Sean wondered aloud. "Is she mad about something else?"

"Is this seat taken?" asked a voice. I didn't even look up. I knew it was Lindsay.

"Sorry. We're kind of busy," I told her.

Sean watched Lindsay walk slowly away, then turned to stare at me. "That was cold," he said, pretending to shiver.

I shook my head. "I'm sure she was going to yell at me about ruining the Secret Santa gift exchange. What am I going to tell her? It wasn't me, it was the restless spirit of a girl who died here sixty years ago. Like anyone would believe that! She'd think I was crazy!"

"Crazier," corrected Sean.

I gave him the stink-eye. "Nice," I said.

Sean thought for a moment. "But what if she was going to apologize?" he asked.

I laughed. "Not a chance," I told him. But when I glanced across the room at Lindsay, I caught her looking at me, her expression sad. I quickly looked away. Now I was the one who was mad. Lindsay should have stood up for me no matter what. I didn't care how bad things looked. I needed her to have my back yesterday and she had failed miserably.

"Maybe there's something Grandpa hasn't told

us, a detail he forgot," Sean said, interrupting my thoughts. "We can ask him."

I shrugged my shoulders. "Sure," I said. "We have nothing to lose, anyway."

After everyone had left to go skiing, we approached Mr. Dowd at the front desk. "So, what else can you tell us about the girl who died here?" Sean asked.

Mr. Dowd thought for a minute. "I've told you everything I know," he finally said.

"Do you know anything about a friend of hers named Eleanor Thomas?" I asked.

Mr. Dowd shook his head. "Doesn't ring a bell. You might want to go to the Snow City library. They have a lot of historical materials. If you want to find information on anyone who lived in this town, that would be the place to go."

Sean had been to the library for story time when he was little, so he knew the way there. We walked along Main Street, the snow crunching under our feet. It had snowed again last night, and the town looked beautiful under a fresh layer of powder.

"Maybe we can find out if either Virginia or Eleanor has any living relatives," said Sean. "Maybe they remember the story and we can find out what really happened and why Virginia's spirit is so unhappy."

"Do you really think we can put her spirit to rest?" I asked.

"Maybe," said Sean. "We may as well try. I feel kind of bad for her. She died so young. She probably never got to do most of the things she dreamed of."

"Me too," I said. "Plus it is supercreepy to stay in a haunted inn. We should fix it for your grandpa."

"He still doesn't even believe it's haunted," said Sean. "But I have a feeling that things are only going to get worse until we figure this out."

"And I'll probably keep getting blamed for it." I quickened my pace. "Let's go!"

The library was an old solid-brick building. We walked up the steps and through the large front doors. Our footsteps echoed on the marble floor. In the children's section, one of the librarians was reading a gigantic copy of *Caps for Sale* to a bunch of preschoolers.

Sean smiled. "Those were the days!" he said.

We found a librarian, a tiny old woman in a pink cardigan, with glasses hanging around her neck on a beaded necklace. "Do you have old newspapers we could take a look at?" I asked. "Like, from the 1940s

and '50s?" She led us over to some rolls of microfilm — almost like old camera film — and showed us how to thread them into the machine.

"May I ask what you are looking for?" she asked.

"We need to find some information on two girls who lived in Snow City back then," I said. "Eleanor Thomas and Virginia Emerson."

"Oh, the Thomases!" she said. "You should have just said so. Eleanor Thomas married Ed Costigan. Their daughter Audrey owns Costigan's Curiosities on Main Street."

Costigan's Curiosities. Why did that sound so familiar? We copied down the address, thanking her profusely for saving us hours of research.

When we got there, I stood in front of the store — the same place that I had gone to with Lindsay and the girls on our first day here. It felt so long, long ago, but it actually had just been a couple of days. "Come on," I said to Sean, who was staring at a photo in the window.

"Look at this," he said to me. It was the same photo of two girls that had caught my eye days earlier.

"Yeah, cute old picture," I said.

"No," said Sean. "It's the girl in the photo. She looks just like an old-fashioned version of you."

I squinted at it. *Really?* I mentally gave the girl a haircut and updated her wardrobe. "Maybe a little," I said. I shrugged. "Let's go inside."

We stepped inside the store and the bell jangled. A middle-aged woman in a funky patterned dress, orange tights, biker boots, and a red cardigan stepped forward. "Hello!" she said. "Welcome to Costigan's Curiosities."

I felt suddenly shy. Was this Eleanor's daughter? Was I really going to tell this woman that we thought that her mother's dead best friend was haunting an old inn because she was still angry about something her mom had done — though we didn't know what — sixty years before? It suddenly sounded completely ridiculous.

Sean started talking first. "That picture in the window . . ." he started.

"Oh, isn't it sweet?" the woman said. "It's my mother when she was twelve years old. Eleanor Costigan. Well, Eleanor Thomas at the time. You want to hear something really funny? You look just like her!"

We both gaped at her.

"Really?" I said.

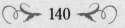

Sean and I looked at each other. We didn't know where to begin.

Finally, I bit the bullet. "Um, has your mom ever mentioned a friend named Virginia Emerson?" I asked.

Sean raised his eyebrows at me. *Talk about jumping right into things*, his look seemed to say.

I thought I saw a shadow pass over Audrey's face. But she shook it off and smiled. "Yes, she has. Why do you ask?"

"It's a long story," said Sean. "My grandpa owns the Emerson Inn. And we've found lots of Virginia's old stuff in the attic. Pictures and notes . . ." His voice trailed off.

"She and your mom seemed so close. And we just want to find out more about Virginia. Do you know anything about their friendship?" I asked.

"Why don't you ask my mom about it yourself?" she suggested.

Sean looked as surprised as I felt. "Oh!" I said. "She's still . . ." I was about to say "alive" but quickly changed it to "living in the area?"

"She is!" she exclaimed. "But she's away for the day." She wrote down an address on a piece of paper. "Why don't you two come over tomorrow morning

at about ten o'clock? You can ask her your questions then."

We left Costigan's Curiosities almost giddy with excitement. We were getting closer to discovering the mystery!

It couldn't be soon enough. When we got back to the inn, Mr. Dowd's face looked grim. He led us into the library.

We gasped. It was in a shambles. Books were scattered everywhere. Several Christmas ornaments had been broken. A few book covers had been torn clear off.

Mr. Dowd bent down and picked up the remnants of an ornament. He looked at it sadly.

"Oh no," said Sean. "Nana's owl."

"Yes," said Mr. Dowd. "What a shame."

He shook his head. "I don't know how this happened," he said. "No one was here."

We knew exactly what had happened. But we also knew that he would never believe us.

We had to figure out how to calm Virginia down before she *really* got mad.

CHAPTER FIFTEEN

"I can't believe we're about to meet the famous Eleanor," I said the following morning.

"I can't believe I'm going to get to see what you'll look like when you're an old lady," Sean said.

"Very funny!" I cried, swatting his arm.

We got a little lost, but soon found the house we were looking for, a cozy little cabin a couple of blocks off of Main Street. It even had a swing on the front porch.

I knocked. A sweet-looking little old lady opened the door. I gave Sean a grin. Old me was cute! "Welcome!" she said. We both stepped inside. The house was as neat as a pin, with overstuffed chairs and a couch laden with hand-stitched pillows.

"I'm Sean, and this is Haley. Thanks for letting us ask you some questions."

"You're welcome!" she chirped.

"What a great house," I told her.

"Thank you," she said. "It's an old miner's cabin, dating back from the 1800s. Come in, sit down." She indicated an overstuffed chair for Sean to sit in.

He sat. *Pfffftttttt!* A loud noise rang out. Sean's face turned bright red.

"Mother!" cried Audrey. She came out of the kitchen, wiping her hands on a tea towel. "Really, isn't it time for you to grow up?" She shook her head. "My mother loves practical jokes. Always has. You have no idea what it was like growing up. Once she packed a snake in a can in my lunch box. Nearly gave me a heart attack!"

She smiled at her mother lovingly. "Never a dull moment growing up with you as a mom, that was for sure."

I exchanged a meaningful glance with Sean. We knew someone else who loved practical jokes, too!

"So, my daughter said you were inquiring about an old friend of mine?" Eleanor asked.

"Yes," I said. "We were wondering what you could tell us about your friend Virginia Emerson."

Eleanor got a strange, sad, faraway look in her eyes. "Ginny and I were the best of friends. We lived right near each other and were in the same class at school. We did everything together. Actually, she's the reason I've always loved playing practical jokes. She had the most creative ideas. We drove her poor aunt crazy! And then one day we had a fight. It was such a silly argument, but I remember it so well. You see, I was invited to a birthday party and she wasn't. She thought I should turn down the invitation, but I really wanted to go. She was furious. She said she would never talk to me again. An entire week went by and we ignored each other." She sighed. "And then one day she didn't show up at school. . . ." Then she told us a story so sad I had to fight the tears from falling. Sean looked grim.

"So that's what happened," she said. "But I have to ask . . . Why are you so interested in hearing about Ginny after all these years?"

"This is going to sound very strange," I told her. "But Sean's grandfather owns Virginia's — Ginny's — old house, the Emerson Inn. And a lot of strange things have been happening. We think . . . we think that the inn is being haunted by Ginny's ghost."

"You're sure you're not playing a joke on an old lady?" she asked.

"We would never do that to you," I promised. "To anyone. That's totally not funny at all."

"We're deadly serious," said Sean.

She looked out the window, a wistful look on her face. She turned back to us. "But what can I do?"

"Do you think you could come tell the story you just told us at the inn?" I suggested. "Maybe if Ginny hears it, it will bring her some kind of peace."

She shrugged. "Okay," she said. "I don't really get it, and it sounds nuts, actually. But you two seem like such nice kids." She pinched Sean's cheek. "And you were such a good sport about the whoopee cushion," she said. "I'll see you at the Emerson Inn tomorrow afternoon."

"Crazy!" said Sean on our walk home. "But it all makes sense — why Ginny went from being a mild presence to an angry ghost. It's the anniversary of her death, you look like her best friend, you played a practical joke. It all makes sense."

"And my best friend and I aren't getting along," I added. "That must have pushed her over the edge."

Sean nodded.

"Do you think we're doing the right thing?" I said worriedly. "I mean, we're messing with the spirit world here. It's kind of scary. And we're bringing Eleanor to meet her dead best friend. I mean, what if she freaks out and has a heart attack or something?"

"I think it will be okay," said Sean. "Did you see how sad Eleanor was when she was telling us the story? This is going to be good for everyone — the living and the dead."

I shook my head. "I hope you're right."

"So, let me make sure I've got this," said Mr. Dowd the next day. "A ghost is haunting this inn and you're bringing her best friend here to talk to her." He grinned. "Well, allrighty, then! My schedule appears to be free this afternoon. Should be interesting." He shook his head. "But I sure hope you kids aren't going to be disappointed."

I was bringing Ginny's scrapbook to the library when I ran into Mackensie and Lindsay in the hallway. They were dressed for a day on the slopes.

"So, what's this I hear about you raising the dead?"

Mackensie asked scornfully. "Anything for attention, huh, Haley?"

"Mackensie!" said Lindsay.

Mackensie turned to Lindsay and narrowed her eyes at her. "You're not telling me you believe this craziness," she said.

"I . . . I don't know," Lindsay replied. "but there's no need to be rude about it."

Mackensie took off her jacket. "Well, I don't know about you, but I wouldn't miss this freak show for the world."

I shrugged. "Go for it," I said. I turned to walk away.

"Haley!" Lindsay called out. "Good luck!"

I spun around, certain she was mocking me. But she looked totally serious.

"Thanks," I said.

The girls followed me into the library. Sean and Mrs. McElhinney joined us.

Lindsay and her mom both looked at me worriedly.

Mr. Dowd brought in a tea tray and a plate of leftover Christmas cookies and set them on the coffee table. "We're all set for our séance!" he said merrily. Mackensie snorted.

I looked at Sean. I wondered if he had the same butterflies in his stomach that I had.

And I wondered if he was thinking what I was thinking. What if our crazy plan didn't work and just made Ginny angrier? What would happen then?

The answer was too scary to imagine.

CHAPTER SIXTEEN

Eleanor took a deep breath before she stepped into the entrance hall of the inn. She looked around and shook her head. "So many memories," she said. "I used to spend so much time here with Ginny and her brother. We used to hide behind this grandfather clock when we played hide-and-seek. We'd sneak into the kitchen and steal cookies from the cookie jar when the cook wasn't looking. We'd explore the basement and pretend that the furnace was a big fire-breathing monster. I haven't been back since that awful day. . . ." Her voice trailed off. She looked very, very sad. Her daughter patted her on the back reassuringly.

I took Eleanor by the hand. "I'm sorry to bring back such sad memories," I told her. "But we're hoping that if you tell your story, it will put her spirit at ease."

Eleanor smiled and looked around mischievously. "So, where is she?"

I walked her to the library. The room was silent. It was already getting dark, so Mr. Dowd lit a fire and placed some candles on the table. I lit a match and set them all ablaze.

Once Eleanor was settled on the couch I introduced her to everyone — Lindsay, Mr. Dowd, Mrs. McElhinney, and Mackensie.

Mr. Dowd poured tea for everyone and passed around the plate of cookies. But everybody looked too nervous to eat. Eleanor looked around the room. "Shall I begin?" she asked.

"Please do," I told her.

"Ginny and I were the best of friends," Eleanor said. "She was so much fun — she so loved a good practical joke."

I could feel Lindsay staring at me, but I didn't look her way.

Eleanor continued, "We were always having sleepovers and playing in my tree house. She lived in this inn with her maiden aunt and brother. Her parents had died when she was young, and she loved

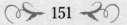

coming to my house and spending time with my family. We were inseparable. Like sisters. We did everything together. Then one day we had a silly fight. A total misunderstanding. I was invited to Mary Hinklebottom's birthday party and Ginny was not. I knew I should have told Mary that I wouldn't go without Ginny, but I heard there were going to be pony rides and I really wanted to go. Ginny felt betrayed. She was so angry she said she would never talk to me again. We ignored each other for a whole week." She shook her head. "If only I hadn't been so stubborn . . ."

I could feel Lindsay's gaze burning into me.

Eleanor stared at the oriental carpet as she spoke. "Then one day she didn't show up at school. My teacher said that she was home sick with scarlet fever. I felt terrible and headed straight to her house after school to tell her I was sorry. But there was a quarantine sign on the door. No one but family members and the doctors was allowed inside. I begged to be allowed to come in, just to see her for a minute, to tell her how sorry I was and how stupid I had been. Finally, the cook came out to send me home. I asked her to tell Ginny I was there and to ask her to forgive me. But I knew the cook was busy and distracted and I always wondered if she gave Ginny my message. And two days later Ginny was dead. I never saw my best friend again.

"I remember the funeral like it was yesterday. Not a dry eye in the house. It started to snow when they lowered her coffin into the grave. And she was gone, forever. I . . . I . . . never got a chance to say goodbye." She began to weep.

A feeling of terrible sadness came over me. Then the hairs on my arms began to stand on end as I felt a familiar ghostly presence in the room. Soon everyone else began to catch on. First the rocking chair in the corner began to sway, slowly at first, then faster. The curtains began to move, even though no windows were open. The lights flickered, and the candles blew out.

Mackensie gasped. Her face was as white as, well, a ghost.

"Ginny?" Eleanor cried out. "Ginny, is that you?" She took a deep breath. "Not a day goes by that I don't think of you. I miss you so." She reached around her neck and pulled a heart-shaped locket from under her sweater. With shaking hands, she opened it. "See, I never stopped wearing our friend-ship locket. Me on one side and you on the other," she said softly. "Best friends forever."

Everyone gasped as the candles suddenly relit themselves.

"This is weird," said Audrey. "Really weird."

Suddenly, there was a strange sliding noise. It was coming from the card table. We all stood up and gathered around. As we stared in disbelief, the Scrabble board tiles began to move, all by them-selves. Mackensie screamed and ran out of the room. Everyone else stood rooted in place, hardly able to believe their eyes.

The tiles formed a message: THNAK YOU HALEY.

There was a gasp, and then shocked silence.

Eleanor laughed. "Ginny never was a very good speller."

CHAPTER SEVENTEEN

"If I hadn't seen it with my own eyes, I'd never believe it," Mrs. McElhinney said, shaking her head. "Look at me, my hands are still trembling!"

I was worried about Eleanor. I mean, it's got to be pretty shocking to realize that your best friend is an unhappy ghost who is still mad at you. But remarkably, she grinned at me when it was all over.

"Well, that was wonderful," she said. "And strange, too. Thank you, Haley. The fact that the two of us never got to say good-bye was the biggest regret of my life. And now we have, thanks to you."

She invited Sean, me, and Mr. Dowd back to her house that night for dinner. She was a great cook and the pranks were kept to a minimum. I did make sure

that the cover on the saltshaker was screwed on tight before using it.

Over chicken with stuffing, twice-baked potatoes, and roasted root vegetables, Mr. Dowd apologized to Sean. "I'm sorry I never believed you," he said. He looked sheepish. "You were right. I *did* buy a haunted inn!"

At breakfast the next morning everyone peppered me with questions. Was it true that we had seen a ghost? What did she look like? Why was she so unhappy? Everyone looked at me with renewed respect.

Everyone except Mackensie. Despite running out of the room in terror, she had somehow convinced herself that it was all a big trick. "You set the whole thing up," she said. She folded her arms across her chest and glared at me. "The things people will do for attention."

This made Sean and me laugh, which annoyed her even more.

Lindsay rolled her eyes. "Really, Mackensie?" she said. "You were there. You saw the whole thing!"

Packing to go home was a lot less organized and a lot quicker without my mom to supervise. I kind of just threw everything in willy-nilly.

My mom would not be proud of me.

But I was pretty sure she'd understand if packing neatly was not my number one priority at the moment. Yesterday had been quite a wild day. I sighed and sat down on my suitcase to get it closed. "It all fits coming but not going!" I said aloud.

There was a knock on the door.

I opened it to find Sean. "Dad and I are about to head out," he said. He shook his head. "What an adventure, huh?"

"The craziest one ever," I said. "Hey — I just wanted to say thank you. You were the only one who believed me."

Sean laughed, embarrassed. "Listen," he said. "It was great to meet you. Maybe we could plan another ski trip after the new year. You don't want to forget your parallel turns."

"That sounds great," I said. "Maybe over spring break."

"Perfect," he replied. "I have an in with the inn-keeper, you know. I think he can arrange it." He paused for a minute, then looked me in the eye. "Listen, Haley, divorce stinks. But don't be too hard on your parents. I'm speaking from experience. This is hard for them, too."

I nodded. "I'm still kind of mad at them for not working things out."

"But you love them. And I'm sure they tried really hard." He sighed. "And there's nothing you can do, anyway. So you've got to make the best of it."

It was good advice. "Thanks," I said.

Sean helped me carry my suitcase down the stairs. On the first landing we stopped and looked at the picture of Ginny and Eleanor. Mr. Dowd had replaced the glass. The two girls smiled out at us, without a care in the world. We glanced at each other, smiled ruefully, then continued down the stairs.

"Well, bye," I said to Sean. He shook my hand, then thought better of it, and pulled me in for an extremely awkward, but totally sweet, hug. My first hug from a boy!

I left my suitcase by the front desk and headed to the library. It was empty. I cleared my throat. "Well,

um, good-bye, Ginny," I said. "I hope you can rest in peace now."

All I heard was complete and total silence. Perfect.

I stopped at the front desk to say good-bye to Mr. Dowd and Harvey. "Thanks for a great trip," I told Mr. Dowd. "It was a visit I'll never forget!"

"I heard I might be seeing you over spring break," Mr. Dowd said. He blushed. "Maybe we'll have dinner with Eleanor while you're here."

"Why, Mr. Dowd!" I said with a surprised grin. Actually, those two would make a good pair!

"Everyone likes a girl who enjoys a good practical joke from time to time," he said.

We both laughed.

"Allow me," he said, picking up my suitcase and carrying it outside to the bus for me.

"Good-bye," I said, and climbed up the stairs. I paused and turned around for one last look at the inn. Then I headed down the aisle, looking for a seat.

About halfway down I spotted Lindsay sitting by the window. I was about to keep going when she looked up. "I saved this seat for you," she said.

"Thanks," I said as I slid into the seat next to her.

"Where's Mackensie?" I asked, craning my head. "I thought she was your *seat buddy*."

"Who talks like that, anyway?" Lindsay said, making a face. "She's sitting in the back. Turns out she is a way bigger jerk than I thought. All she cares about is clothes and boys. It was fun at first, but then it got boring. And she doesn't want friends, she wants followers who go along with anything she says!" Lindsay shook her head.

I suppressed a grin.

"Please don't say *I told you so*," she begged me.

"I won't," I said. "I'll just *think* it."

"I can't begin to tell you how sorry I am about everything. . . ." she started to say.

I held up a hand. "No apologies necessary," I said. "If we've learned anything on this trip it's how important best friends really are. And how stupid it is to hold grudges."

Lindsay grinned at me gratefully.

"Oh, I have something for you!" I squealed. "You never got to open your Secret Santa gift in all the craziness."

Lindsay's mouth fell open. "That's totally right." She clapped her hands. "I can't wait!"

I pulled the gift out of my backpack. After all this time, it was looking worse for the wear. The wrapping paper was creased and the ribbon bedraggled. Lindsay tore open the wrapping paper eagerly.

She held a small leather-bound book. On the front in gold script it said *Friends Forever.* She flipped open to the first page. There was a picture of the two of us from preschool. Lindsay had on one of her famous mismatched outfits — kneesocks, white sandals, purple plaid shirt, and yellow-and-orange striped skirt. I was in a denim dress, clutching my Tinky Winky.

"This is awesome!" she said. I had saved a friendship's worth of movie stubs, tap-dancing programs, class pictures, and birthday cards and compiled the highlights into one beautiful book, if I do say so myself.

Lindsay hugged the book to her chest. "I love it, Haley. It's the best gift ever."

She took a deep breath. "So, I've got to know . . . how did you first discover that the inn was haunted? You've got to tell me everything!" She paused and bit her lip. "Unless it's too upsetting for you to talk about . . ."

The bus rumbled to a start and with a squeal of the brakes, pulled away from the curb. I smiled. I had learned how to ski, made a new friend, and gotten an

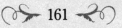

old one back. Plus, I'd helped two estranged friends find peace. I'd learned that being a part of the popular crowd didn't really interest me. It had been quite a trip. And now I was ready to stop running away from my family problems and head home.

"Well, it all started when we first pulled up in front of the inn," I said. "It was cute. It was quaint. It was decorated with sparkling Christmas lights. And for some strange reason, a chill ran down my spine. There was something weird about that inn. I tried to shake it off, but I couldn't ignore it for long."

Lindsay shivered. "I had no idea!" she said. "That sounds terrifying."

"It was pretty scary," I admitted.

"A ghost!" Lindsay said. "I'd never have believed it if I hadn't seen it with my own eyes. What a crazy story." She shook her head, then fished into her backpack and pulled out a white paper bag. "Sour Patch Kid?" she asked.

I smiled and stuck my hand inside. "I thought you'd never ask," I told her.

BITE INTO THE NEXT POISON APPLE,
IF YOU DARE....

HERE'S A SPINE-TINGLING SNEAK PEEK!

"Let's play a game!" Chloe suggested.

"Truth or dare!" Kimmie and Alyssa chorused.

"Classic slumber party game!" said Taylor, giggling. "Okay, I'll go first." She turned to Chloe, smiling. "Truth or dare?"

"Truth," said Chloe.

"Okay." Taylor's hand rested on the crystal choker and suddenly her tone became deadly serious.

"Truthfully, of all the people in this room, who do you consider your closest friend?"

Chloe blinked. "Huh?"

"Out of the four of us," Taylor clarified, "who do you like most?"

What a loaded question! Why would Taylor put her on the spot like that? The truth of course was that Sam was Chloe's best friend; she had been since first grade. But to say it out loud, in front of Kimmie and Alyssa and even Taylor, would be just plain rude.

Was it too late to switch to dare? Chloe wondered.

"Well?" Taylor prompted, her eyes flashing in the fiery glow. "You have to answer. Those are the rules."

Even though it was freezing outside, the blazing fire — and the horrible question — were making Chloe sweat. "Phew, that fireplace throws off major heat!" she said. Stalling for time, she pretended to be occupied with pushing up the sleeves of her fleece pajamas.

"Now that you mention it, it is kinda warm in here," Taylor agreed. She stood up to unwrap her thick chenille robe, and as she did, the clasp of her choker snagged on the loopy material. As Taylor tugged off the bathrobe, the choker dropped from her neck, landing with a jangle on top of her sleeping bag.

"Oops!" She bent to pick up the necklace, which she tossed into the closet. "Okay, back to the game. Where were we?"

"You just asked Chloe who her best friend is," Alyssa reminded her.

Taylor frowned. "I did?"

The four other girls nodded.

"Well, you don't have to answer," Taylor said apologetically. "I'm sure I was just goofing around when I asked. It's a dumb question. I totally take it back!"

This seemed peculiar, but as far as Chloe could tell Taylor was being completely sincere. She let out a deep sigh of relief.

"Somebody else go," Taylor suggested.

"I will," said Kimmie, turning to Alyssa. "Lyss, truth or dare?"

"Dare!" Alyssa grinned. "And make it a good one!"

"Okay! I dare you to go, all by yourself, down those spooky old back stairs that lead to the dark, empty kitchen, and . . ."

Alyssa gulped. "And?"

"And . . ." Kimmie's face broke into a huge smile, "bring me the rest of the pepperoni pizza!"

"Oh, man!" said Alyssa. "I thought you were gonna make me do something terrifying!"

"That *is* terrifying," Chloe noted. "For Kimmie's stomach! She already ate five slices of pizza, half a bag of nacho chips, three brownies, and a cookie."

Kimmie grinned and fluttered her eyelashes. "Can I help it if I have an extra-fast metabolism?"

Alyssa squirmed out of her sleeping bag and set out on her mission. Two minutes later she'd returned not only with Kimmie's pizza, but also the nacho chips and cheese puffs, a bottle of grape soda, and the remaining brownies.

"My turn," said Sam. With a determined expression, she turned to Taylor. "Truth or dare."

"Truth!"

Sam looked as if she'd been hoping Taylor would pick that option. "All right," she said in a frank tone, "be honest. How did you know that Chloe would find her yellow cardigan in Evie's laundry? And what happened to Adriana Faulker that kept her out of school today?"

Chloe's eyes went wide. Alyssa let out a tiny gasp. Even Kimmie froze, pizza slice hovering in midair halfway to her mouth. They couldn't believe Sam had just asked those questions. But they were all glad she had.

"Don't forget," said Sam with a solemn nod. "The name of the game is *truth* or dare."

For a moment, Taylor said nothing, looking from one curious face to the next. After what seemed like forever she shook her head. "I seriously have no idea what you're talking about."

"Just tell us," said Chloe. "We promise we won't be upset!"

"Tell you *what*?" Taylor turned up her hands, her brow knit in confusion.

"If your choker has powers!" Kimmie blurted.

"Yeah," Alyssa chimed in. "Is it . . . magical? Enchanted? Or radioactive? Just spill it. What's the deal?"

"Magical?" Now Taylor's eyebrows shot upward in surprise. "Enchanted?"

Actually, a much darker word was floating around in Chloe's mind: *cursed*.

POISON APPLE BOOKS

The Dead End

This Totally Bites!

Miss Fortune

Now You See Me...

Midnight Howl

Her Evil Twin

Curiosity Killed the Cat

At First Bite

THRILLING.
BONE-CHILLING.
THESE BOOKS
HAVE BITE!

ROTTEN APPLE BOOKS

Mean Ghouls

Zombie Dog

UNEXPECTED.
UNFORGETTABLE.
UNDEAD. GET BITTEN!